# memory
# minefield

# memory minefield

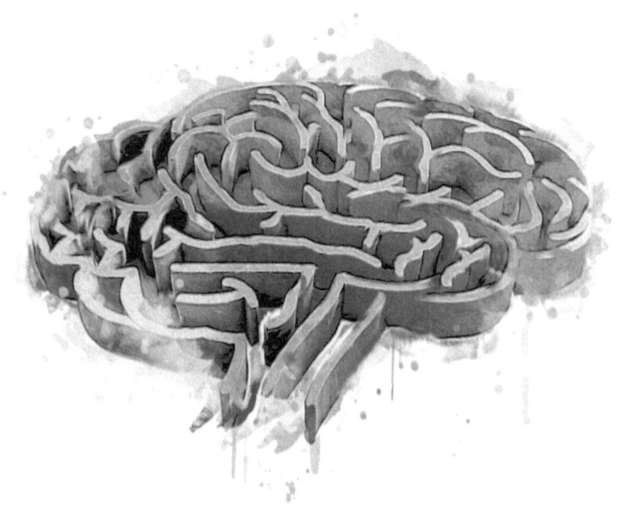

## mel torrefranca

Lost Island
PRESS

**Lᴏst Island**
—— P R E S S ——

Memory Minefield
Copyright © 2022 Mel Torrefranca

All rights reserved. No part of this book may be reproduced or used in any
manner without written permission of the copyright owner except in the
case of brief quotations embodied in critical articles and reviews.

Library of Congress Control Number: 2021924658

ISBN 979-8-9850102-1-3 (paperback)
ISBN 979-8-9850102-0-6 (ebook)

This book is a work of fiction. Names, characters, places, and incidents
either are the product of the author's imagination or are used fictitiously.
Any resemblance to actual events, businesses, companies, locales or
persons, living or dead, is entirely coincidental.

Lost Island Press LLC
Oro Valley, AZ
lostislandpress.com

In loving memory of James Hensley

# ari

On a strange November afternoon, I woke up with my eyes already open.

I was sitting on a furry beanbag in my bedroom with an incomplete psychology worksheet on the desk in front of me.

*The hippocampus, a brain structure responsible for learning and memory, is located in which part of the brain?*

After skimming the four possible answers, I circled *B—temporal lobe.* Only then did I notice the blood dripping from my fingertips.

With a sharp gasp, I dropped my yellow pencil and extended my right arm to get a clearer view of my wounds. The feeling of warm blood trickling down my palm dissipated as I realized that my nails were simply coated in a pomegranate-colored polish.

*Weird.* I relaxed my shaky hands, resting them by the worksheet on my desk. *I don't remember painting them.*

My eyes widened as I read the name *Ari Cortez* in the corner of the page. *I don't remember anything at all.*

I sprung from the beanbag, stumbling to face the middle of the bedroom and nearly falling in the process. With heavy breaths, I searched for a dangerous face—for the villain who had made me a stranger in my own body.

But I was alone.

The bed in the corner had a burnt-orange duvet cover peeled back as though someone had been sleeping there a matter of hours ago. Against the opposite wall stood a dresser that matched the mahogany wood of my desk—its drawers half-open, overflowing with warm-colored fabrics.

I took a few steps forward and caught a glimpse of movement through the corner of my eye. My head shot over my left shoulder just in time to catch a stranger's face staring at me through a window.

At first I assumed that the girl was another person, but when my fingers met with the curly brown hair resting on my shoulders, the girl in the glass reached for her hair too.

*It's not a window.* My heart rate settled as I walked toward my reflection, the girl in the glass copying me in sync. *It's a mirror.*

Our dark eyes met like we were two separate entities crossing paths, infatuated with the matching patterns of freckles on our faces, yet also afraid of such a strong coincidence.

"Hello?"

Although I'd seen the lips of my reflection move, I struggled to believe that the foreign voice had been my own. I pressed my fingers against my hot neck—the skin right under my chin—and spoke again.

"Hello?" I said, louder this time. My vocal cords vibrated in confirmation.

Desperate for something less creepy than this mirror to focus on, I parted from the glass to discover a collage above my desk that I'd been too stunned to notice earlier. A collection of film photos and handwritten quotes had been taped onto the wall with thin strips of decorative tape.

I recognized my own face in the photos. In some I'd even been wearing the same outfit I wore now—brown linen pants, a cream t-shirt, and a golden necklace chain with a seahorse pendant. The faces accompanying mine varied, but it didn't take long to spot a pattern.

Apart from myself, the only consistent character was a blond girl with wide blue eyes. Her hairstyle changed dramatically from photo to photo—

straight to curly, long to short, up to down—but her plaid jacket and sparkly smile never changed.

I squinted at the message written on the only photo of us two alone:

*Stop thanking me. I'm always here for you.*

The message on the photo implied that the girl in the plaid jacket had somehow helped me in the past. Perhaps the necklace I wore also had something to do with her, because my fingers fumbled instinctively for the seahorse pendant that dangled against my shirt.

*It's like I grabbed it out of habit.*

I shook my head and let go of the necklace before yanking open the first drawer of my desk. There had to be something hidden in this room that could help me understand why I'd lost my memories.

Inside the drawer I found a short stack of papers marked with scattered numbers, words written so sloppily I could hardly read them, and—in a much higher ratio than the two previously mentioned—lines and lines of endless scribbles. I spread the pages across my desk, grabbed a random page, and brought it toward my nose to study the markings closer.

*Looks like a bird's-eye view of a building.*

My eyes jolted to the door as footsteps echoed from another room, heading in my direction. I stumbled left and right, my eyes flying from wall to wall in search of a place to hide—but before I could part from my desk, the footsteps came to a halt.

"Sweetie?"

The door swung open to reveal a woman in a flowing teal dress. Her tender smile loosened my tight grip on the page.

"Did I hear you call?" she asked.

I opened my mouth to speak, but when the woman's eyes landed on the floor plans spread across my desk, the smile tumbled off her face, and the words got caught in my throat. With every step she took in my direction, the air grew colder.

"I thought you were done with this, Ari."

I stumbled away from her, wincing as my back slammed into the wall.

The woman whom I assumed was my mother snatched the page from my grip, and I held my palms out in front of me, lips trembling.

"What..." I stammered, the words struggling to leave my throat. "What happened to me?"

My panic must have been contagious, because her jaw dropped, and the mountainous folds across her forehead settled into flat land.

"Oh no. No, not you too." The corners of her lips twisted downward into a pout as she said, "You've forgotten."

I couldn't tell if she was asking a question or making a statement.

"I believe so." I crossed my stiff arms, an attempt to cloak the defensive guard I still wasn't willing to let down completely. "But why?"

My mother glanced at the page in her hand one final time before pulling me away from the wall and into her suffocating embrace.

"We'll work through this together," she whispered into my ear, "okay?"

And although working through *this*—whatever that vague word represented —wasn't exactly a concern to me, her soft voice eased my stress, and I finally let my guard down. The mystery of why I didn't remember myself vanished, my confusion morphing into pure curiosity now that I wouldn't have to solve this alone.

"What did you say I was done with?" I asked.

She stepped away from me and raised her brows.

"I was holding that"—I pointed at the paper in her hand—"and you said you thought I was done with something."

"Done with procrastinating on your homework to draw these floor plans." She pulled at one of my curls and released the strand to watch it recoil. "You've always dreamed of becoming a structural engineer."

For a moment I thought I was experiencing nostalgia—that when I was younger, my mother would tug gently at my curls as a form of endearment —but after she gathered the other papers from my desk, I decided that the childhood memory was nothing more than a lie my longing mind had made up for comfort's sake. The result of a desperate attempt to fill the void that had once held real memories.

"Let's talk in the living room." My mother grinned, but I could tell by the unsteadiness of her voice that she was holding herself together for my own sake. "I'll explain everything, okay?"

I uncrossed my arms, and my lips formed a straight line as she left through the doorway.

Listening to her footsteps echo down the hall, I wondered why she hadn't left my sketched floor plans behind, especially if those pages had once played a role in my passion for structural engineering. I wondered why the only paper remaining on my desk was the worksheet I had woken up solving.

My eyes wandered to a wrinkled page in the collage on the wall, and for the first time, I spotted something familiar—a quote I remembered by heart.

*Knowing yourself is the beginning of all wisdom.*

"Aristotle," I whispered without even a moment of thought.

And as I read the quote again, I felt an unexplainable certainty that my mother had lied.

---

On Sunday, the day after I'd woken up, the television ran all day long to keep my parents and I updated on the latest memory loss case analytics. For three days people of all ages all over the world had been mysteriously waking up with no recollection of whom they were.

And I happened to be one of them.

My mother and father spent hours flipping through albums of my baby photos and sharing funny stories from my past. I knew they were trying to help me understand myself better, but the guilt completely infested me. If anything, my parents were the memory loss victims, not me. They were the ones grieving over the old Ari.

*I wish there was something I could do to lift their spirits.*

That painful helplessness only intensified when they introduced me to Stella Pierce.

The girl stood in the entryway of our home that evening, a mere cutout of the photos I'd seen of her on my bedroom wall—plaid jacket and all. According to my mother, Stella was my best friend, and she also happened to live right across the street.

Stella ran from the entryway, my father shutting the door behind her as she wrapped me into a hug so tight it rivaled my mother's. The fabric of her scratchy jacket—still cold from the November air—left me with a desire to experience the chill myself. I hadn't left the house since I'd woken up, but I was too nervous to ask my parents for permission to. They were still in the realm of strangers, possibly approaching the acquaintance zone.

"Oh, Ari. I'm really, really sorry." Stella's long, blond hair made my neck itchy—but she smelled like roses, so that evened out the discomfort. "I'll tell you everything you need to know. I promise."

She stepped away from me before I had the chance to hug her back, not that I'd ever felt inclined to.

The four of us sat around the square dining room table that evening, the air dangerously quiet. My parents and I had eaten nothing but packaged crackers and granola bars since I'd woken up, so this was our first proper meal together, and none of us knew how to act.

I made brief eye contact with Stella and my parents before resorting to staring awkwardly at the table, which was a bit too small for us. Our feet nearly ran into each other, and the mismatched plates and platters covered every spot on the tabletop. I pushed my tall glass of lemonade away from the edge, scared of accidentally knocking it over.

My father eventually cleared his throat. "Feel free to dig in."

I reached for the serving spoon sitting in a white bowl of creamy chicken.

"Some believe that certain people, experiences, or objects might help bring back lost memories," my father explained as I scooped a helping onto my plate. "I thought we might give sweet lemon chicken a try. It was your all-time favorite."

My parents glued their eyes to me as I brought a forkful to my lips, waiting for a sign that consuming my favorite food had brought the old Ari back.

Stella cringed as I swallowed my first bite.

"Tastes good," my father asked, "right?"

I nodded dramatically to convince him that I enjoyed the dry chicken breast smothered in sickeningly sweet, lemony syrup. But as I stabbed my fork into a second piece of chicken, the glimmer of hope in his eyes faded, and he proceeded to spoon out his own serving.

I counted each painful bite in my head, promising myself to tell my father I was too full to finish after my tenth.

*Is he lying to me, or did I actually like this?*

Stella had no issue devouring the sweet dish, and I wondered if waking up had somehow messed with the part of my brain responsible for taste.

"Is Ari coming to school tomorrow?" Stella asked my parents, her mouth stuffed with chicken.

My father glanced at my mother before sighing. "I don't think so."

*School.* I swallowed my fourth bite. *I haven't even thought of it.*

Stella set her fork down, and by the mere volume of the *clink*, I could tell she wasn't satisfied with my father's response.

"You can't keep her locked up like this, Mr. C." Stella crossed her arms. "She's gonna have to go back to school eventually. Don't you see that you're both more afraid than she is?"

I continued choking down my lemon chicken in solitude. Apparently no one wanted my opinion on the matter, but I didn't mind. If they had asked me whether I felt ready to attend my first day of school, I wouldn't have known what to tell them.

"Stella, I completely understand what you mean," my mother said, "but it's only been one day. Ari needs time to heal, and—and you're right about being scared. We need time to heal too, okay?"

For the first time today, a smile broke onto Stella's face—the same smile I had seen countless times in the film photos on my wall.

"Just one day, Mr. and Mrs. C." Stella pointed a finger in their direction. "That's all I'm asking. One day, and if it's too overwhelming, you can homeschool Ari for all I care."

My father's posture loosened as though a weight had been lifted from his shoulders. He pointed back at Stella playfully, and I got a sense that he was used to dealing with her challenges. Perhaps the hint of familiarity excited him.

"Deal, but let's wait a week first," my father said. "Until then, maybe you can start by showing Ari around town. If she's feeling up for it, of course."

*Which I'm definitely feeling up for*, I wanted to say, but I was far too shy to express my enthusiasm.

Fortunately, I didn't have to wait long to fulfill my dream of leaving the house. After Stella had returned home from school the following afternoon, she knocked on our front door to invite me on a walk with her.

"Are you feeling up for it?" she asked.

I smiled so widely it left my cheeks sore.

Contrary to what my parents had believed, exploring the outside world wasn't the least bit overwhelming. I hadn't lost any knowledge-based memories, so I still knew that benches were for sitting on and that most birds have wings to fly. The information overload they thought I'd experience never came, and instead I found myself in a state of awe.

*I wonder if the old Ari loved autumn as much as I do.*

Dead leaves decorated the cracked sidewalks of our old town like blotches of red ink, and colorful dogwood trees sprouted from the ground every direction I turned.

*Is that snow?* I squinted at a white-tipped mountain in the distance.

Stella pointed out all kinds of places, like the historic Pentaware Art Museum and the peaceful McCloud Park. There weren't too many people out on the sidewalks—perhaps because the overcast sky threatened to rain at any moment—but the strangers who passed us all made the effort to smile. I found myself with a raging curiosity to learn everything I could possibly learn about this charming town I called home.

"And that over there is Damon Academy." Stella pointed at a brick building to our right. The school logo—a golden raven's head inside an emerald-green circle—hung on the gable above the front doors. "It's an all-boys school. They have some of the highest test scores in Oregon."

"That sounds impressive." I pinched my numb nose to warm it up. As beautiful as the scenery was today, the autumn air sure was brutal.

"Oh, it's impressive, and they definitely know it." Stella walked faster, her sneakers crunching against the fallen leaves. "Rule of thumb—never trust a guy from Damon."

It wasn't until we entered our neighborhood on the way home when I finally gathered the courage to ask Stella one of the many questions circling through my head.

"On my wall I found a photo of the two of us," I said. "I think it was you who wrote it. The note said to stop thanking you."

"Did it really?" Stella asked in a monotone voice.

"Do you know what I was thanking you for?" I looked at her, but she avoided my eyes, staring blankly at the empty road next to us. "It seemed important."

"Not sure." Stella shrugged. "I helped you study for an algebra test once, so that might have been it. You've always hated math. Not your best subject."

I frowned at my boots, the memory of the papers I'd found in the drawer of my desk flashing through my mind. I'd nearly forgotten about them.

"But I thought I wanted to be a structural engineer. Doesn't that require math?"

"An engineer?" Stella finally made eye contact with me, and this time, her smile was genuine. "God, no. Ari, are you kidding me? Music, photography, boring museums—that's your kind of thing. Not engineering."

It became clear in that moment that I couldn't trust anyone but myself to uncover my past. My mother might have lied to me about my dream career, my father might have lied to me about my favorite dish, and Stella might have lied to me about that photo on my wall. The issue was that at least one of them was lying, and there was no way for me to determine who was telling the truth. Perhaps none of them were.

*But if I can't find the old Ari through the people around me, is there any way for me to find her at all?*

By the time Stella and I stopped at the front steps to my house, her smile was gone. She wrapped her arms loosely around me, and for the first time since I'd woken up, my eyes watered. Stella had lost her best friend, and she'd spent two days trying to find her.

But I didn't know if I could help.

Stella could play the role of my best friend, yet it was nothing more than that—a role. We were only actors in a play based on the past.

"Bye, Ari." There was a tremor in her voice, yet despite her obvious gloominess, I could sense a remnant of hope that I could change—or in this case, *revert*.

Stella backed away from me and tucked her hands into the pockets of her plaid jacket. She was about to head across the street to her house, but something over my shoulder caught her eye.

"What's that?"

I scanned the front doorstep but saw nothing out of the ordinary.

"There, that thing." Stella pointed at a bush to the left of the front steps. "Is that a letter?"

I probably wouldn't have noticed the envelope tucked in the bush had Stella not pointed it out, and the next few weeks would have been a lot less messy that way. But instead of shrugging away my curiosity, I reached between the frost-coated leaves to retrieve a slightly damp envelope.

Apart from my name, which had been spelled out across the front in black sticker letters, there was nothing else written on the envelope. No return address—not even a stamp.

Stella joined me by my side. "Who's it from?"

I paused, hesitating to open it in front of her.

"I wrote it this morning." The lie slipped from my tongue effortlessly. "It's a letter for myself. My mother heard on the news that it might work as a possible treatment."

"Really?" Stella spoke louder than usual, my words rekindling the flame of hope within her that had nearly died out. "Ari, that's great!"

I sighed. "Doesn't seem to be working."

"Well, you never know, so just keep doing what you can. I'll see you tomorrow afternoon?"

I nodded, and Stella parted from my side.

As soon as she crossed the street and entered her house, I ripped the envelope open.

*If the letter doesn't have my address on it, that means the person who wrote it likely delivered it to my house themself.*

I pulled out the paper inside to reveal a printed message.

*Dear Ari Cortez,*

*I hope this letter finds you well. I heard news that you've lost your memories, which must be a pain. Luckily, I know what you have to do to get them back.*

*In the Pentaware Art Museum you'll find a painting titled Seahorse by the deceased artist M.L.C. Steal the painting during the next full moon, and your memories will return as soon as you leave the building.*

*This is not a threat, but a kind suggestion. Whether you put this plan into motion or not is up to you, but keep in mind that this is a one-time opportunity for you and you alone. I wish you the best.*

I blinked at the page a few times before folding it and stuffing it back into the envelope.

*Who would write something like this? And how do they know where I live?*

The idea that stealing a painting during a full moon could somehow restore my memories sounded like magic, but then again, who was to say that magic wasn't responsible for me losing my memories in the first place?

*No.* I shook my head. *That's impossible.*

But as I stared at the distant buildings to my right—where the Pentaware Art Museum was located—my fingers reached for the seahorse pendant pressed against my chest. The cold autumn air left my body shivering, yet my mind felt warm and comforted.

The wind ruffled my curls, and for the first time since I woke up, I smiled.

*How bizarre.*

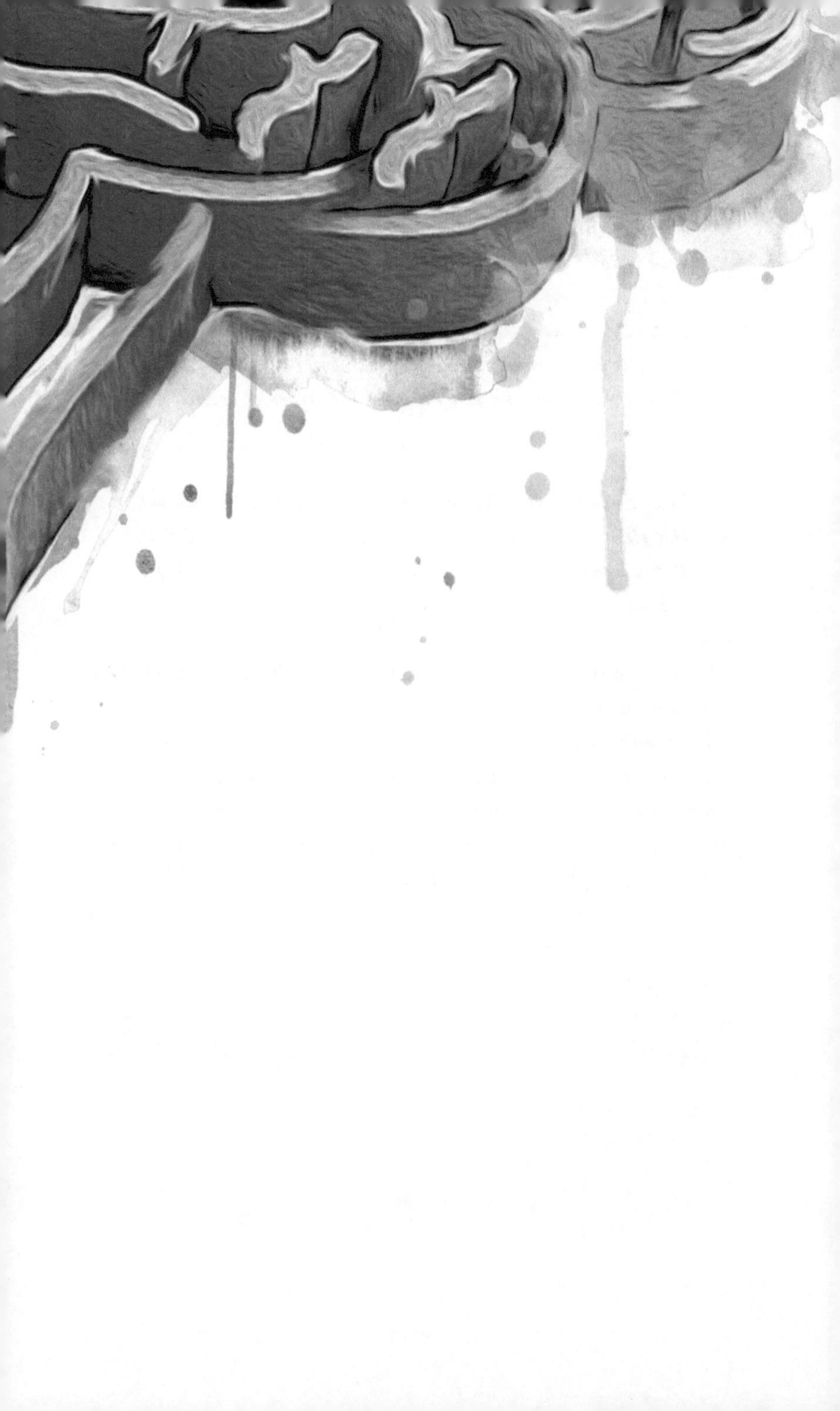

c h a p t e r  2

# j e r e m y

If you're looking for a primary source to quote in your research paper, you've come to the wrong place. The seven-day memory loss pandemic still remains a mystery, and I'm the last person to ask for trustworthy information about the phenomenon. I'm just a guy who happened to get wrapped up in the chaos that unfortunate November.

I know my intentions don't justify what I did, but I still think it's important to share that I never meant to cause any harm, or to be funny, or to mess with medical research. My goal was simply to land some quick cash, and that was all there was to it.

Okay, maybe that wasn't my only motive, but it's what I told myself at the time.

The day it all began—I remember it clearly. It was Wednesday, November 17th, the sixth day of what would soon be referred to as *Remembrance Week*.

Ironic, I know.

People all over the world had been losing their memories, and although cases would trickle off indefinitely the following day, we didn't know it at the time. In the eyes of every passing face, I read the question, *What if I'm next?* We all shared the same horrifying worry that cases might not stop until the entire world had undergone a memory reset. Our doctors, teachers, parents, children—all unable to remember anything about themselves.

I was scared of losing my memories too, but it was a different kind of fear that isolated me in the Damon Academy library during lunch break that Wednesday. While the other guys tossed around conspiracy theories in the dining hall, I sat on a forest-green velvet chair with actual facts spread across the table in front of me—articles I'd printed from the internet, scientific papers our teachers had assigned for us to annotate during class, and newspapers I'd snatched from my elderly neighbor's doorstep this morning.

Don't judge me. She never read them anyway.

The rain trickled against the side of the building as I read through another boring article. My nose scrunched up, the smell of artificial lavender really pushing my patience.

*I think I'd prefer the scent of a rotting corpse.*

I would've complained to the librarian, but she was napping on a sofa in the corner, and even my heart wasn't black enough to interrupt a sleeping soul. I had no right to complain anyway. Most school libraries suck, but apart from the nasty air freshener our janitor used, the library at Damon was actually pretty nice. The tall paned windows to my left provided a great view of the duck pond at McCloud Park, and an abundance of tables and chairs filled the spacious aisles between bookshelves. Normally the room would be buzzing with boys studying for tests, but today students were more concerned about chatting with friends while we all still remembered each other.

The front door to the library creaked open, and my eyes froze at the sound of my brother's voice.

"Jeremy?"

I continued reading the page in my hands, hoping Isaiah would do a quick scan of the room before deeming it empty, but his footsteps only grew louder. He stopped at the end of my aisle, peering between the two rows of bookshelves to find me flipping to the next page of the article my groggy brain only half-understood.

"Still going at it?" Isaiah took a seat across from me and rested his arms on the table. His navy blue blazer left a trail of water on the wood, which meant he'd likely gone outside in the rain to look for me, but my pride was too high to appreciate the gesture.

"You don't have to be here." I set the useless article aside and reached for a newspaper.

"Don't be silly," Isaiah said as I raised my chin to face him. "I wanna help."

My brother grabbed a few pages and scanned them as though he actually cared about curing Rei's memory loss. I knew he wasn't helping because he considered Rei a friend of his—he was helping because he knew that losing Rei had been rough for me. Isaiah's fake compassion was nothing but indirect pity, and I got a sickening impression that he thought I couldn't handle anything without him.

I shook my head, breaking off my frustration and turning back to the newspaper in my hand. I'd been searching for a sign—a pinch of hope that Rei might get his memories back someday. That a researcher was on the verge of a scientific breakthrough. But so far, I had nothing.

Over the weekend the memory loss phenomenon had been hilarious to my friends and me—including Rei. We didn't see it as a problem because we never thought it would affect us. Cases were reported in cities we'd never been to and countries we'd never heard of.

But then Rei lost his memories on Sunday night, the third day of Remembrance Week, and our jokes weren't funny anymore. It was real now. We knew a memory loss victim from our own town in our very own high school.

I never had the chance to say goodbye to Rei—not even after he lost his memories. His dad had first pitched the idea of moving to Iowa months ago, to which Rei had resisted harshly, but without his memories, Rei no longer had a reason to stay. By Monday morning he was already on a long drive to Des Moines with his dad, vanishing from Pentaware with no recollection of me.

I felt like Rei died on Sunday, but unlike the dead, he didn't have a gravestone to leave behind.

I found myself skimming words without actually reading them, so I pinched my arm to wake myself up. I could feel my heavy head drifting, the sleep deprivation from the past two nights finally catching up to me. I'd spent hours watching the television alone downstairs, clicking through different news channels in hope of hearing something positive about the memory loss victims instead of endless case reports, interviews, and depressing analytics.

My eyes skimmed the phrase *Genetic Variables* in the header of one of the newspaper articles, and I jumped out of my seat.

Isaiah stared up at me. "Did you find something?"

I leaned over the library table, hoping I hadn't misread the header.

*Reported Overnight Cases Peak on Tuesday Morning, Doctors Speculate Genetic Variables at Play*

"No way," I muttered.

"What does it say?"

I read the text aloud, my voice growing louder with every word.

"*Researchers race to discover the true cause of mass memory loss. Although various theories exist, many believe an unknown virus may be responsible and that symptoms only emerge for those with a certain genetic marker.*" My lips morphed into a grin for the first time in two days as I caught sight of an ad at the bottom of the article. "And listen to this! *Cognitive psychologist Amara Singh offers one thousand dollars to memory loss victims who volunteer to undergo three hours of testing.* And this Dr. Singh is based here, in Pentaware!"

Isaiah peeled his eyes from me, his focus drifting to the window as the rain intensified.

"Hello? Are you even listening?" I waved the newspaper in front of his face, and he swatted my hand away before standing from the table.

"A local psychologist." Isaiah crossed his arms and leaned against the bookshelf behind him. "So?"

"Imagine how much money we could get!"

I could tell by the folds on his forehead that he wasn't a fan of another one of my schemes, but I continued anyway.

"Think about it. Two *identical* twins with *identical* genetics, but one has memory loss and the other doesn't. That debunks the most popular theory. This doctor might even pay us a premium."

"No."

Normally when Isaiah would tell me a blunt *no*, I would listen, because my brother was pretty much always right when it came to determining whether my plans were overboard or not. But today I wasn't going to let such a huge opportunity slide between my fingertips.

"If she decides to test both of us," I said slowly, "that's two thousand dollars. After pooling our earnings together with your savings from work, we'll have enough for a new car."

Isaiah's gaze drifted to the droplets of water racing down the window. "A new one?"

I couldn't care less about pulling up to school in a nicer ride, but Isaiah had been embarrassed of our shared fifteen-year-old sedan since the day our dad passed it on to us. My brother was too afraid to bring up the topic of a new car with our parents, so he'd landed a job at the Pentaware Art Museum to start saving up for one himself. He had some weird status obsession, but today his weakness was my advantage, so I didn't judge.

I ripped the ad from the bottom of the local newspaper article—which included Dr. Singh's address—as the bell rang to mark the end of lunch.

"We can head there after school," I said, tucking the ad into the pocket of my blazer.

Isaiah narrowed his eyes at me as I hauled my canvas rucksack from the floor onto the table, unclipped the main compartment, and crammed my scrambled papers inside. The thrill was already starting to lift my spirits— my energy returned as though I'd had a full night's rest. I swung the heavy rucksack over my shoulder like it weighed nothing.

"We really shouldn't."

"That's obvious." I headed for the library door, the smile on my face widening. "But what's stopping us?"

Isaiah chased after me, his damp sneakers squeaking against the hardwood floor.

"Hey, hey!" He caught up to my side and peeked over his shoulder, making sure the librarian was still asleep. She was, but he lowered his voice to a whisper anyway. "Fine. I'm in, but only if you agree to stop after this. No more risky plans. This is the last time that—"

"Yeah, yeah!" I replied, mocking his panicked tone. "Deal."

---

The door swung open, barely missing our noses.

"Hello?" Dr. Singh looked back and forth between us, wisps of raven-black hair falling from her half-collapsed bun. "How can I help you?"

Just looking at her drooping eyelids and dull complexion nearly made me yawn, but I quickly remembered my role as a memory loss victim and pulled the same blank expression I'd seen on victims' faces during interviews.

Isaiah cleared his throat. "I—uh—well, this is my brother." He set a hand on my shoulder a bit too dramatically, leading me to flinch, and I wanted to do nothing more than kick his shin for being so ridiculously obvious. "He lost his memories last night. We saw your ad in the paper."

Dr. Singh's tired expression vanished instantly, her face brightening like a night light in a child's bedroom. She pulled an extremely fake smile and ushered us inside.

*What a bland room.*

To our right was a wide desk covered in coffee-stained pages, empty canned espressos, and a speaker blasting classical music. Apart from her cluttered desk and a few chairs, there was no other furniture in sight, which left an awkward amount of empty space. The only piece of decor was an oil painting that hung by the door to a separate room of her office.

Dr. Singh plopped herself onto a seat behind her desk and clicked a button on the speaker to pause that horrid piano music. When Isaiah and I sat on the guest chairs across from her, she smiled even wider, and it was starting to creep me out. If I hadn't been suppressing my emotions to play the role of a memory loss victim, my brain would've activated fight or flight mode. Absolutely guaranteed.

"I'm Isaiah," my brother said, his voice shaky. "And this is…"

Isaiah's eyes wandered to the oil painting on the wall to our left. Various shades of blue joined forces to form an elegant horse underwater, but in place of its two hind legs was a fishtail. Some kind of half-fish, half-horse hybrid. I personally thought its strange factor overpowered its beauty.

"It's a reproduction of a piece in the Pentaware Art Museum," Dr. Singh said, following his gaze. "Do you like it?"

Isaiah nodded, studying the painting with fascination. I had to fight myself to keep from rolling my eyes.

*That museum he works at has turned him into an art freak.*

"Sorry." Isaiah cleared his throat and gestured to me, peeling his eyes from the painting. "This is my twin brother, Jeremy."

Dr. Singh nodded and turned to me, her smile fading. Thankfully.

"How are you, Jeremy? Can you tell me how you woke up?"

It took me a moment to realize what she meant by *woke up* in the first place. People had started using the term to describe the moment memory loss victims forgot about their pasts, which wasn't usually while waking up from sleep. Based on the articles I'd read and the news reports I'd watched over the past few days, a majority of memory loss victims woke up while performing everyday tasks.

I made up a story about how I'd been playing video games at home when I'd suddenly dropped the controller and couldn't remember where I was. She jotted notes onto one of the million yellow notepads in front of her before asking Isaiah for his side of the story.

Surprisingly, Isaiah's nervousness played in our favor. My brother had always found dishonesty challenging, but from Dr. Singh's perspective, his fidgeting fingers and wandering gaze must have appeared as symptoms of sadness or regret, because she nodded at him with pursed lips and slightly raised brows. When he finished explaining how he'd found me in the living room looking around, Dr. Singh made a weird humming noise, perhaps to be comforting or something, and responded with, "I can imagine that must have been difficult. So how's two thousand each?"

I nearly grinned.

"Sorry," Isaiah said. "What do you—"

"I think it'd be best to study both of you for comparison. Nothing major —just an MRI scan and a few written psychometric tests." She reviewed her scattered notes. "If published, the results will remain anonymous, but if we go through with this deal, you have to promise not to do testing for anyone else. If asked, you were volunteers, found the testing experience stressful, and no longer want to be treated as lab rats for minor medical advancements. I'll give you four thousand dollars for your time."

I could hardly believe it. Dr. Singh was willing to pay double to test the two of us exclusively.

"Is that legal?" Isaiah asked.

I was supposed to have my memories erased and therefore lack an ability to care about this testing thing at all, but I couldn't help it. I gave Isaiah my death stare, but more of a toned-down version so Dr. Singh wouldn't notice.

"Cash." Dr. Singh held her hand across the desk. "It'll be our secret."

Her words slapped the morals right off Isaiah's face. He took her hand and shook it, but his gaze was on that horse-fish painting again.

Dr. Singh led us into the other room of her office, which was filled with all kinds of cool-looking medical equipment I didn't know the purpose of. After Isaiah and I took turns in a claustrophobic chamber for a ridiculously long amount of time, she gave us multiple written tests with mathematical word problems easy enough for an elementary student to solve.

> *What percentage of crimes were related to pick-pocketing or burglaries?*

I scanned the pie chart next to the question, which clearly showed that pick-pocketing made up twelve percent while burglaries made up nineteen. I circled *C—23%*. Surely it wouldn't hurt to make my condition more convincing on paper.

Soon enough four hours had passed, and our testing was finished. Dr. Singh led us back into her boring front room and rummaged through her desk drawers for our payment.

"Great, you're all set." She held four sealed envelopes toward Isaiah like a magician would hold out a deck of cards to choose from. "A thousand per envelope."

Isaiah stepped forward, but he didn't take the money. He froze, likely feeling guilty, but after four hours with Dr. Singh, I was not willing to leave empty-handed. I passed my brother and reached for the money myself.

Dr. Singh's grip on the envelopes tightened as I wrapped my fingers around them, stopping me from taking the money. She pursed her lips as our eyes met.

*Don't panic*, I reminded myself, quoting what Rei had told me during our first scheme together. *It's panic that gets you caught.*

Rei and I had met during English class as high school freshmen—a little over two years ago. We had both rolled our eyes at a guy in class with blue hair who wouldn't shut up about his summer internship in Paris. He even made fun of guys who had never been on a plane before, and considering how Rei and I had never been on a plane before, we were pretty pissed off.

Rei caught up to me in the hallway after class with an idea so crazy I burst into laughter. Really, I thought he was fooling with me.

*"I'm making a quick stop at the principal's office,"* Rei said. *"I'm gonna tell him I saw that blue-haired kid drown a duck at McCloud."*

When Rei didn't laugh with me, my humor faded into concern. *"Oh... you're serious?"*

He scoffed at my response before making a quick turn toward the office.

I morally couldn't watch a classmate get expelled from Damon for such a silly lie—especially not on the first day of school—so I followed Rei, pleading for him to reconsider.

Rei stopped at the entrance to the principal's office, and I stood a few feet behind him, staring at his back as he finally responded to my blabbering.

*"Don't panic."* Rei set his hand on the doorknob. *"It's panic that gets you caught."*

I stumbled into the principal's office after Rei, but he started speaking before I could drag him back into the hallway. I listened in horror while he explained that we had *both* seen the blue-haired boy drown a duck in the pond at McCloud Park.

Was it a ridiculous story? Yes. But did Rei sell it?

Let's just say our blue-haired classmate had an extremely awkward check-in with our principal about his mental well-being. And who knew all it took to pull off something like that was to play it cool?

So as Dr. Singh held her stern gaze on me, I turned off my paranoia and continued doing what I had grown extremely skilled at doing over the past two years.

I put on a show.

Tilting my head to the side, I pretended like Dr. Singh's odd reaction had left me confused.

And eventually, just as our principal had done, Dr. Singh dropped her doubts about the story she'd been told. Her face softened as she released the envelopes, and I took full control of the money.

"Oh! Before I forget..." Dr. Singh reached for one of her yellow notepads and held it toward Isaiah. "Can I get your number? I'd like to be in touch in case I have any follow-up questions."

"Of course." Isaiah's fingers shook as he grabbed a pen and scribbled his number onto the notepad.

During the drive home, Isaiah wouldn't stop stressing over the possibility of Dr. Singh finding out.

"What if she sees something in those MRI scans?" He gripped the steering wheel tight enough to choke a grown man to death. "If something gives away the fact that we lied, I bet she'll track us down and demand we give her the money back."

I tuned him out, counting the cash in my hands. I had never held so many hundred-dollar bills before, but the excitement of our scheme had worn off, and I hated how I wasn't happy.

You've probably guessed it at this point, but I never wanted the money —or a new car, for that matter. All I wanted was a distraction. Scamming Dr. Singh was simply a band-aid for the wound, but now that distraction was gone. Ripped away. Unless I could find myself a new band-aid, the wound would never heal.

Sure, I had other friends at Damon Academy, but spending time with them was so predictable. We'd study together, spout the same mediocre inside jokes, and occasionally discuss our dreams for the future. In middle school that'd been enough for me—just as it remained enough for Isaiah now—but Rei had woken me up to how fun life can be when you bend the script once in a while. Like when you compliment a cashier or high five a teacher.

For a moment I thought I might text Rei. He likely still had the same number, as well as my contact information and all of our previous text conversations, so there was a chance he'd be willing to stay in touch. But the thought of rebuilding our friendship from scratch exhausted me, so I pushed the idea away.

Isaiah took a deep breath after his guilty monologue, and the silence drew me back into reality.

I slipped the money into their original envelopes. "You done?"

"Look, I know you're not gonna like this, but I *really* think we should bring the money back."

"After all that? No way."

"I already have eight grand saved up, and I'd rather keep working than buy a new car with stolen cash." He paused. "I just—I thought doing something you'd normally do with Rei might help you accept that he's really gone."

*Oh.*

It made perfect sense. My brother had never ratted me out, but he'd never joined in on my plans either. I thought he'd finally caved in because I'd discovered his weakness—money for a car. But that wasn't it. This entire day had been nothing but a pity fest.

"You know, maybe it's a good thing that he's gone. He was kinda—you know—"

"What?" I turned my cheek to him, staring at the road ahead of us. "Rei was *what*?"

Isaiah shrugged. "He was a bad influence."

What Isaiah didn't understand was that Rei and I were each other's distractions, and our pranks were simply a byproduct of our time together. When Rei came up with the idea of lying about our classmate drowning a duck, his parents were going through a messy divorce. I was Rei's distraction then, and he was my distraction after my parents left Isaiah and I home alone on our birthday to get dinner with coworkers. But with Rei gone, who would be my distraction now?

Isaiah pulled into the driveway and took a deep breath before twisting the car key. The rumbling came to a stop.

"I know this isn't easy," he said in a soft tone, "but you're not alone. Really."

And then I messed up.

I did something so wrong, so horrible—but at the time it felt so right, like there'd been a flaw in the system, and I'd flicked the switch to make everything function correctly again.

"What do you mean?" I asked, my voice trembling as the cold air seeped into our car.

I was hoping he'd feel embarrassed for being sappy and would finally leave me alone. I didn't need him spending his lunch breaks looking after me when I knew he'd much rather be laughing with our friends in the dining hall. I didn't need his pity.

If Isaiah would just leave me alone, maybe time could be my band-aid.

*But is that really what I want? To move on like Rei died when he's still alive, finding himself a new group of friends in Des Moines to form new memories with?*

Isaiah searched my eyes—his brows crawling closer together—and I could tell he wasn't planning to leave me alone anytime soon.

"You haven't forgotten anything," he said, "have you?"

I shot him that same blank face I'd pulled for Dr. Singh to poke fun at his ridiculous assumption, but Isaiah didn't catch on.

When his face drained of color, I nearly broke the act to tell him I was joking, but I didn't.

I held that expressionless face.

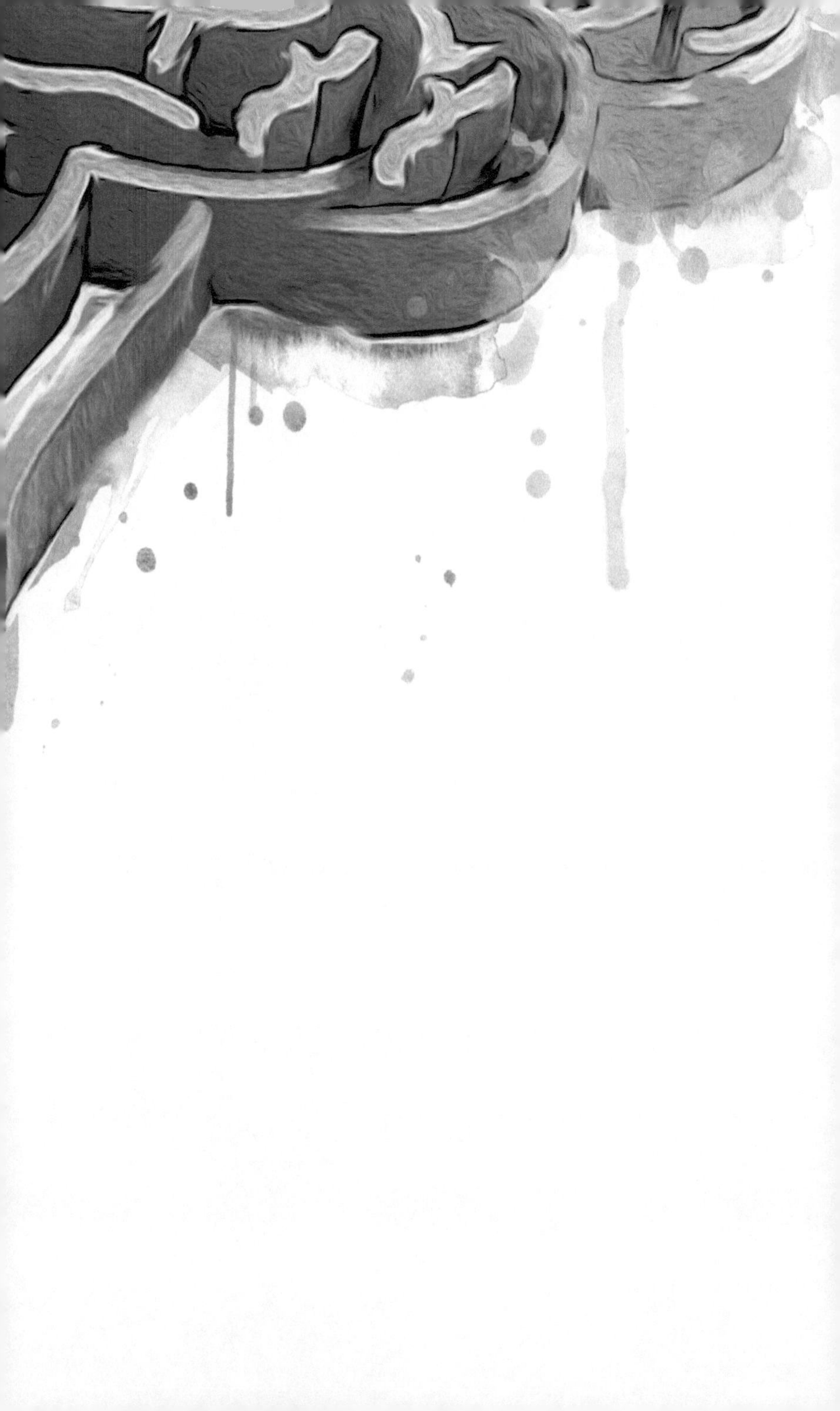

# ari

The memory loss phenomenon, after surging for seven full days, had ended as abruptly as it'd begun, the last reported cases taking place on Thursday evening. Although most people celebrated no longer having to fear losing their memories, I wasn't sure whether I should've been thankful for humanity's sake, or frustrated for my own. I was part of half a percent of the worldwide population affected by what was now officially named *Remembrance Week.*

I'd been left responsible for solving a jigsaw puzzle of the past, but I didn't even know where to find the first piece.

On Saturday afternoon, exactly one week after I'd woken up, I stood in the narrow hallway of our home in front of the one room I hadn't explored yet. My parents hadn't mentioned or entered this room even once, and I couldn't sit around wondering why any longer.

I tried to twist the doorknob, but it wouldn't budge.

"It's a mess in there."

My hand jumped from the doorknob, and I spun around, gasping like I'd been caught with blood on my hands at a crime scene. My mother stood at the end of the dark hallway, her shiny eyes on the door I'd failed to open.

"Sorry." I bit my lip, hoping my mother wouldn't assume I didn't trust her. She'd been extremely kind and accommodating, and I couldn't imagine how hurt she'd be if she knew the doubts I had regarding her honesty.

"It's a storage room. For old furniture." I spotted a warmth in her tone, as though she'd once held fond memories of the items now tucked away. "Let's get going, okay? You're already late."

I nodded, glancing at the locked door one final time before following my mother down the hallway and into the living room, where my father stood with car keys in his stiff grip.

As part of the Mental Health Initiative Act, the government had begun rolling out memory loss counseling programs, usually held at public schools or libraries. My parents had discovered that Pentaware was included in the handful of locations hosting the first programs, and it just so happened that the nearest teen group would meet at the Pentaware High School gymnasium every Tuesday and Saturday afternoon—a mere two-minute drive from home.

*I'm not ready for this.*

I clenched my fists, trying to will myself to speak against my parents—but failing. Last night I'd passed by their bedroom door to overhear them discussing whether or not I should attend today, so I could tell they were truly passionate about making the right choice for me. The least I could do in exchange for their effort would be to grant them a little trust—despite how challenging that was.

None of us uttered a word until the car pulled up to the front curb of Pentaware High School.

"Good luck, sweetie. Just be yourself," my mother said as I stepped out of the car. "Well, I mean—"

"Thank you, Mother," I cut in, perhaps a bit too harshly.

*I know my memory loss has been hard on my family, but that doesn't mean I should trust them mindlessly.* I shut the car door and turned around, listening to the engine chuckle as my parents drove away. *Why does my heart tell me they're hiding something?*

I watched my biker boots as I walked up the cracked concrete steps, careful not to crush any of the orange and black milkweed bugs crawling around.

The front door to Pentaware High School had been propped open with a wooden stopper, allowing the wind to enter the hallway as it pleased. I zipped up my mocha-colored puffer jacket and stepped inside the cold building, eyes darting around the empty hallway. The dented maroon lockers, flickering lights, and stained floors resembled a location from a horror film, and I found myself walking twice as fast as I normally would.

I sighed with relief as I stopped in front of a door with a silver sign labeled *Gymnasium* hanging on the wall next to it. But when my fingers hovered over the lever door handle, the anxiety of entering a room with strangers started to eat at me again, and the idea of staying in this dreary hallway didn't seem horrible anymore.

*It's okay.* I shut my eyes. *I can do this.*

Unlike the high school students I'd have to face this Monday, the counseling group members were going through the same challenges I was. Surely I could find comfort in the fact that this was a new experience for all of us.

*I might even meet someone who received a letter too.* I opened my eyes, my fingers finally wrapping around the doorknob. *But what if I don't? What if the opportunity in that letter really is just for me and me alone?*

I'd discovered the letter on Tuesday evening, nearly four days ago, and I still hadn't decided whether I should pursue its instructions or not. From my online digging, I'd discovered absolutely nothing about M.L.C. apart from the fact that they'd named their painting incorrectly. The photo I'd found of *Seahorse* online depicted not a realistic seahorse, but an underwater horse with a fishtail in place of its hind legs known in Greek Mythology as a *sea-horse*—with a hyphen between both words.

On one hand, stealing M.L.C.'s painting could be the key to getting my memories back—but on the other hand, it almost felt like a trap. Like a lie. And after constantly questioning whether my parents and Stella were being honest with me over the past seven days, there was nothing I despised more than the concept of being lied to.

"Are you here for the meeting?"

For the second time today, I jumped around to find someone watching me. The girl had a ruby-red dress draped over her dark skin, and her tight ringlets trailed down to her waist.

I nodded and dropped my chin to avoid eye contact. The girl was wearing leather Mary Jane shoes paired with long white socks, which I recognized as an uncommon style choice. It was strange for me to think such a thought, and I started to wonder whether the old Ari had an interest in fashion. Perhaps that would've explained my color-coordinated dresser drawers.

"Me too," she said. "Let's go in together."

I wiped my sweaty palms on the sides of my fleece pants before facing the door again and finally pushing the lever handle.

The dull ceiling lights paired with the tinted windows left the gymnasium with a much darker vibe than the invitingly bright room I associated with the word *counseling*. A volleyball net was still set up from a previous practice, and next to it was a circle of metal folding chairs, more than half occupied.

As the girl in the red dress closed the door behind us, a man from the circle of chairs gestured for us to join them. He had a sticker on his white polo that read, *HELLO MY NAME IS EMMETT.*

I walked toward the circle, my boots squeaking against the polished tangerine-orange floors. When the girl in the red dress and I sat next to each other in two of the empty seats, I counted a total of ten chairs, yet only nine pairs of shoes.

*Are we still waiting on someone?*

My gaze fell directly over Emmett's head as I raised my chin to read the digital clock on the wall behind him. When the time shifted from 3:34 to 3:35, the man cleared his throat as though he'd decided to only wait five minutes for our missing member before commencing the meeting.

"You know what?" Emmett clapped his palms together, drawing the attention of every eye in the room. "Let's get started. I'm Emmett, the assigned counselor for the teen group here in Pentaware."

In a single explosive motion, Emmett stood from his seat—perhaps for dramatic effect. The chair scraped across the gymnasium floor beneath him, shocking the hazy filter out of our eyes. He seemed to enjoy the attention.

"Why don't we start by sharing our name, age, and one fun fact. I'll go first." Emmett stepped forward, deeper into the circle. "My name is Emmett, I'm twenty-five, and I may not look the part, but I have a slight obsession with chess." He stepped back into the rim of the circle, sat, and gestured to the boy sitting next to him.

The redhead to Emmett's right stated his name and age, but when he reached the last task, his raspy voice broke as he said, "I don't think I have any fun facts."

"Oh, of course you do," Emmett said, bobbing his head. "I'm sure there's *something* fun you've learned about yourself since you woke up."

The boy ran a hand through his fiery hair, trying to think of something to say. I could tell he was uncomfortable, and part of me almost wanted to speak up and tell Emmett to leave him alone—after all, what did Emmett know about memory loss? But I lacked the courage.

Just a few minutes into this meeting and my pessimistic view of memory counseling was already crawling back into my head.

But then the redhead spoke again, tossing me out of my frustration.

"I guess I like blue," he said, sparking a few smiles among the circle of new faces, including my own. "I own a lot of blue things." He reached into the pocket of his jacket and pulled out a phone with a sky blue case. Now that he mentioned it, I realized that even his flannel was made of different shades of blue.

*I wonder what my favorite color is.* I studied my dirt-brown pants and faded tan boots. *Earth tones, maybe?*

The introductions made their way around the circle, but instead of paying attention to the names I would inevitably have to remember, my brain wandered as I tried to recall the most frequently recurring colors among my bedroom decor.

Soon enough the girl to my left was introducing herself—meaning I was up next. I'd been so distracted by the redhead's fun fact that I hadn't even decided on my own.

"I'm Piper," the girl I'd entered the gymnasium with said, straightening the frilly straps of her dress. "I'm fourteen, and a fun fact is that my room is filled with crime novels. Practically made of them. It almost looks like I was planning something myself."

The room waited until she laughed before laughing back.

Piper faced me, and I straightened my posture, nervous under the heavy weight of the circle's eyes.

"Uh, I'm…"

I trailed off as the eyes shifted from me to the closed gymnasium door.

Two male voices spoke over each other in the hallway, but I couldn't make out what they were saying. When their muffled conversation came to a sharp halt, the door swung open to reveal a boy with short almond-brown hair and a grin so nervous it made *me* nervous. He was wearing a pair of black jeans with a plain t-shirt—the kind with a little pocket by the chest—and he had his bare arms crossed in response to the chilly air of the unheated building.

When the man next to him—whom I assumed to be his father, judging by their shared olive skin tone—disappeared from the door frame, the boy finally stepped into the gymnasium.

"I'm glad you could make it." Emmett gestured for the approaching latecomer to join us. "We saved a seat for you."

The boy eyed the eight of us victims, searching for a familiar face—not that he'd remember us anyway. His curiosity left me wondering if I'd known anyone in this room before Saturday. It was likely that most of the students here also attended Pentaware High School. Perhaps they'd shared classes with me before. Perhaps we'd even been friends.

The latecomer sat in the empty seat to Emmett's left and started fidgeting with the end of his army green t-shirt, which wouldn't stop curling at the seam.

"We were just introducing ourselves," Emmett said. "Why don't you share your name, age, and a fun fact about you?"

Emmett made eye contact with me and raised his pointer finger, signaling that he'd come back to my introduction later. I wasn't at all annoyed with the extra time to mentally prepare.

*Fun fact*, I thought to myself. *What should I say?*

The boy raised his head slowly, and the sight of his quivering hazel eyes sent a chill down my spine. He was more nervous than I'd been a moment ago, and judging by the argument with his father in the hall, he definitely didn't want to be here any more than I did.

"I'm Jeremy Sargo," the boy said, his chin lowering as his focus reverted back to the end of his t-shirt. "I'm sixteen, and I..."

Folds formed between his eyes as he struggled to choose a fun fact. I got the impression that he was afraid of messing up, like he was facing a multiple choice question that he knew there was only one correct answer to.

Emmett must have had the same impression, because he reassured Jeremy by saying, "It can be anything."

"Well..." Jeremy stopped fidgeting with the end of his t-shirthis hands settling in his lap. "I like coffee."

The circle was dead silent, but when Emmett broke out with a borderline-aggressive smile, everyone else followed suit, their smiles growing as they turned to face me with wide eyes.

I took a deep breath, feeling less anxious after Jeremy's train wreck of an introduction.

"Ari Cortez. I'm also sixteen." I paused for an awkward period of time before remembering that I was supposed to share a fun fact. "I like—I *think* I like photography. I have photos on my wall. And a film camera on my nightstand."

After the final two students introduced themselves, Emmett divided us into three groups of three. He placed me in a group with Piper and Jeremy, and I figured it simply had to do with the fact that all three of us had shown up late. We dragged our chairs from the circle to our own little spot a few feet away, forming a triangle.

The three of us smiled at each other, but we ended up sitting in silence, our eyes on Emmett as we waited for him to share further instructions.

"These will be your discussion groups for the next month." Emmett stood where the middle of our larger circle used to be. "Why don't we start with one simple question?"

I bit my lip, anticipating that his question would be anything but simple. "Who was I?"

His three words left me completely dumbfounded, lost in thought as everything I'd learned from my parents and Stella over the last week spun through my head. Apparently the other members weren't having as much of a hard time, because a humble chatter spread softly through the air, and once it slid into our group, Piper wouldn't stop talking.

"I think I have a pretty good idea of who I used to be. My room is filled with a crazy amount of hints, as well as my phone, but the best part is my diaries." She waved her hands around as she spoke, and I wondered whether she was doing it intentionally or out of habit. "I've read every single entry in all three and a half diaries at least five times by now. I discovered all of my favorite foods, funny memories, and darkest secrets. Turns out I'm also sarcastic, but I'm working on that one."

Although I had a suspicion that I'd eventually grow tired of Piper's talkative nature, I must admit that I appreciated her ability to speak confidently, as though her words required no thought at all. I, on the other hand, could hardly comprehend Emmett's question in the first place.

Who was I? Well, the old Ari had done an awfully great job at keeping that a secret.

Piper cleared her throat, waiting to continue until after I'd raised my chin to prove my attentiveness.

"Don't you think it's weird how I still write exactly the same? I compared my current handwriting to the one from my recent journal entries, and it's identical. I guess that does make sense though, since we didn't lose our muscle memories." Piper rubbed her forehead. "But my handwriting makes me wonder what other parts of myself I haven't lost. I'm sure part of the old Piper is still in here, and I'm determined to find her."

I shifted my attention to Jeremy, hoping that it'd cue him to start talking next. I needed more time to think of something to say.

"I guess it was pretty easy for me to figure out who I was." Jeremy shrugged carelessly, but I could tell from the shakiness of his voice that he felt anything but careless. "My brother has been telling me all kinds of stories about myself, and I'm sure he knew me better than anyone else. But there have to be things I knew about myself that no one else knew—not even my brother. Unless I have a shot at getting my memories back, I guess I've lost that part of me forever."

His slight hopefulness about getting his memories back left me wondering if he might have been sent a letter too. Or maybe part of me was simply hoping that I wasn't in this alone—that I wouldn't have to make this decision to steal a painting as the only person involved.

"Yeah, that'd be convenient." I tried to fight off the urge to ask about the letter. "But do you really think there's a chance we might be able to get our memories back?"

"Probably not," Jeremy said.

"It'd be so nice if someone could just send me a letter," I hinted. "Or some kind of instruction book with steps on how to get my memories back, you know?"

Jeremy nodded, but his eyes were on the floor, and I knew at that moment that no one had sent him a letter.

"Oh, I wish." Piper laughed at the seemingly abstract idea I'd proposed. "Although maybe I wouldn't want a letter like that. In a way, trying to piece together my past is kinda fun. It'd make a pretty good fiction plot."

As Piper blabbered on about the interesting stories she'd read in her diaries, a surge of adrenaline coursed through me. My eyes widened as I remembered a crucial detail from the letter that had flown completely over my head.

*Of all the paintings in the museum, why did the letter specify the one titled Seahorse?* I reached for the seahorse pendant dangling against my shirt. *This necklace I've been drawn to it since the day I woke up. What if it's a sign that I can't let this opportunity slip away?*

I could either steal the painting or not, and if I chose not to, I'd forever have to deal with wondering who I'd be if I had. I'd forever have to live with the haunting question, *Did I lose my one chance to bring the old Ari back?*

Regardless of whether or not the letter's promise was true, wouldn't ignoring the instructions be an unnecessary risk? If there was even a sliver of a chance that stealing the painting could bring my memories back, how could I sit around and wait for this opportunity to expire?

For the past few days, I'd been scrambling to find the missing bits and pieces of my past. I'd been dealing with the guilt of hurting those who cared most about the old Ari. Getting my memories back would be in everyone's best interest. I could ditch my guilt and learn the full truth about who I used to be, my parents could get their real daughter back, and Stella could reconnect with her best friend.

"What's that?" Jeremy pointed at the pendant trapped in my grip.

"I don't know." I dropped the seahorse pendant, hoping he'd drop his curiosity too. "I can't remember."

"You should ask your family or something," Piper said.

I shook my head. "I can't."

I thought back to the day before yesterday, when I'd asked my mother why we didn't have any family photos on display. The walls of every room apart from my own were completely barren, as though someone had walked through and ripped away every piece of hanging decor, leaving behind nothing but small holes that once held nails.

*"We don't like clutter,"* my mother had explained. *"We tire of decor quickly."*

But what I didn't understand was why my parents would store old furniture behind locked doors.

My mother, father, and Stella had all been supportive, but there was no way for me to discern their truths from their lies. I was walking in the old Ari's world with a blindfold on.

It wasn't until Piper suggested I talk to my family about the pendant when I finally realized why I'd been so unquestioning—so distant.

"I don't know who to trust," I added, more to myself than to Piper. "Either everyone's lying to me, or the old Ari was lying to everyone else."

The murmuring of the room filled our circle until Jeremy leaned forward, scaring it away. "Why would you think that?"

"I keep running into contradictions." I finally raised my head, my eyes hopping between him and Piper. "And I'm starting to worry that I'm living a lie."

It was nice to finally open up to people who understood what I was going through. People who had woken up during Remembrance Week, just as I had. Perhaps the eight other memory loss victims in this room were the only people I *could* trust.

"I see." Jeremy leaned back in his seat, his eyes drifting to the windows. "But sometimes you have to live a lie to figure out who you are."

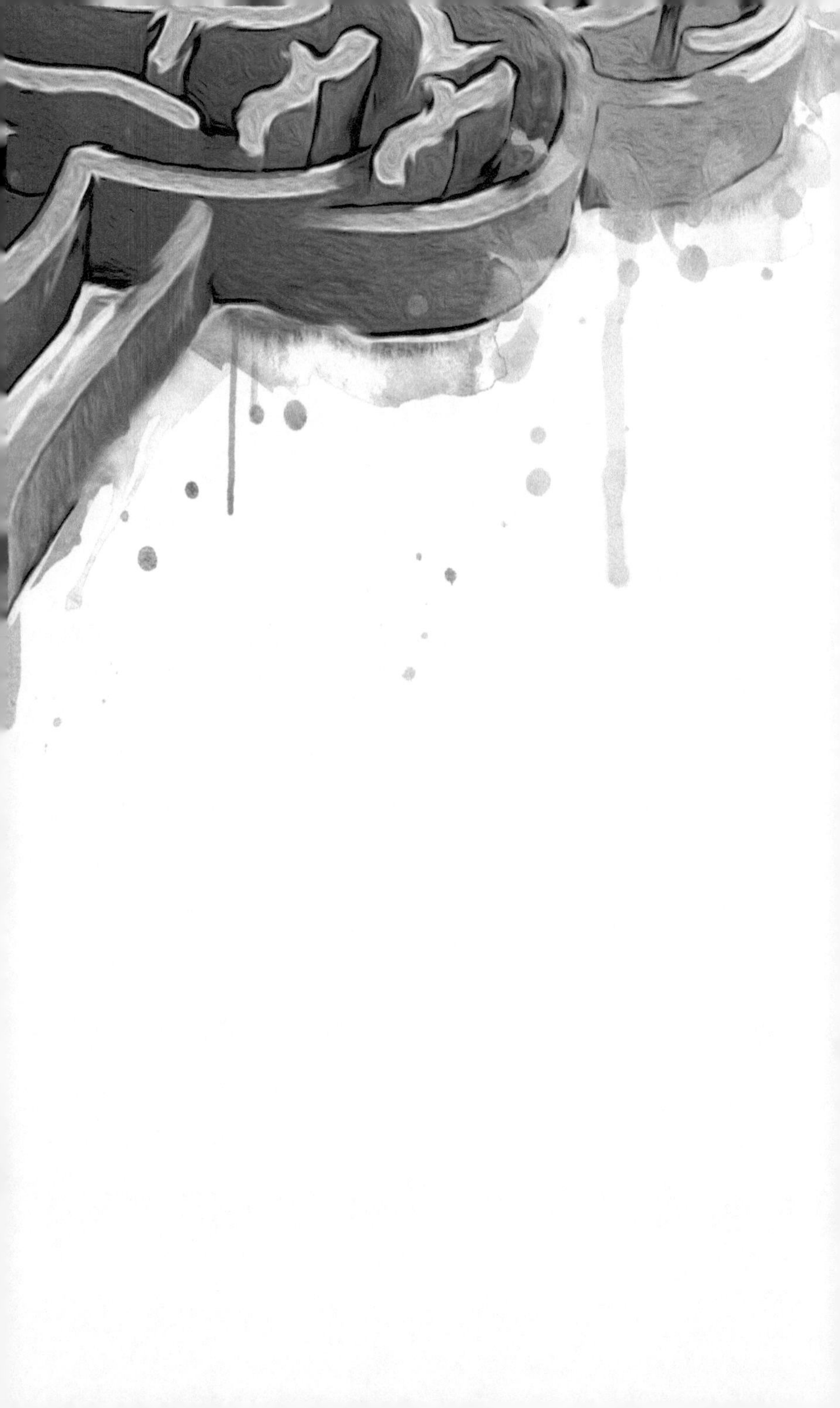

# chapter 4

# jeremy

I know what you're thinking.

*Oh Jeremy, what a manipulative moron you are.*

And you're completely right for thinking so. I knew that what I'd done was wrong, and I knew that I'd have to come clean eventually. But sometimes the consequences of honesty outweigh the consequences of maintaining a lie.

The evening we'd scammed Dr. Singh, Isaiah had dragged me into the house, shouting about my memory loss at the top of his lungs. The looks on my parents' faces had been far more heart-shattering than the temporary frustration I'd seen countless times after they'd heard of another one of my poor decisions.

Isaiah raced upstairs, and our mom chased after him. I wasn't given a moment to speak before our dad wrapped me into his warm embrace.

*"It's going to be okay,"* he whispered. *"You're safe here."*

Our parents had always been busy with work, leaving Isaiah and I with the freedom to live our own lives without much monitoring. Although Rei had never expressed it clearly, I got a sense that he'd envied me for growing up in an upper-class family with two parents still madly in love with each other. But at least Rei had a dad who cared enough to scold him whenever he got caught for another silly scheme. At least his dad wouldn't wave money around to make Rei's repercussions go away.

Instead of easing my dad's stress by telling him that I'd been messing with Isaiah in the car, I hugged him back even tighter. His concern for me was unexpectedly touching, and it was nice to know that beneath his cold persona, he truly cared. I couldn't bring myself to spoil such a sweet moment.

So I didn't.

My parents had taken Thursday off work to introduce me to my favorite restaurants and movies. With every passing hour, I told myself it'd be the last before sharing the truth, but it never was. By the time Thursday evening rolled around, my lie had been running for a total of twenty-four hours. I knew that if this were to go on a moment longer, there was no chance my family would ever forgive me.

*It's been nice, but it's time to call it quits,* I thought as I lay in my bed, unable to fall asleep. *I'll tell Isaiah first.*

But as soon as I parted my lips, Isaiah slipped out of his bed and left our shared room.

I didn't see him cry, but I know he did, because he did that annoying thing where he'd go into the bathroom and leave the sink running for a really long time. So as I listened to the water stream uninterruptedly, I closed my mouth and shut my eyes. The truth would hurt my family more than my lies already had.

I'd gone too deep.

Now it was Saturday, three days after I'd pretended to wake up. I walked down the sidewalk after our first memory counseling meeting with goosebumps on my arms and a million thoughts that wouldn't shut up. The air was bitingly cold today, and I'd been stupid for not grabbing a jacket earlier, but I guess I deserved the discomfort considering the mess I'd gotten myself into.

*If my parents find out now, it'll be worse than if they didn't care about me.* I rubbed my forehead, my mind flashing with every one of my failed attempts to reveal the truth over the last three days. *If my parents find out now, they'll hate me.*

I had no choice but to live with my lie, but now that I'd have to attend these counseling meetings twice a week, keeping my memories a secret wouldn't be easy.

According to the articles I'd read, memory loss victims had lost their episodic memories—the kind associated with specific, movie-like recollections of the past. Procedural and semantic memories—responsible for muscle memory and retained knowledge—were for the most part unaffected among tested victims. I'd watched a viral online video about a piano prodigy affected by Remembrance Week who didn't remember a single lesson from her music teacher but could still play just as elegantly.

Although distinguishing the types of memories seemed simple enough, my extreme paranoia consumed me. I had spent nearly half an hour at the meeting stressing over whether someone had seen me lean over to tie my shoe. It wasn't until I saw a girl from another discussion group tie her own shoe when I'd finally settled down.

I felt like I was walking through a minefield. All it would take was one wrong step for the other members to see through my facade—and then everything would explode in my face.

I crossed the silent street without bothering to check for cars, smiling at the sight of my favorite coffee shop ahead of me.

*But thankfully, I found a fix.*

In the final ten minutes of the counseling meeting, an idea had struck me. An idea that would eliminate not only the risk of slipping up in the counseling group, but slipping up anywhere at all. It would ensure that no one would ever find out what I'd done, and it would ease my guilt for stooping so low.

I'd immediately texted my dad to let him know that I'd be walking home —that I'd made a friend. Considering how badly he had wanted me to attend today's meeting, I knew he'd believe my lie. People fall for lies easily when they want to believe them, just as I had fooled myself into believing that Rei's memories would return—that he'd someday show up here in Oregon again.

I pulled open the sliding oak door to Fire Roasters, and a wave of heat from the cozy coffee shop washed over me as I entered. My numb nose and cheeks burned as they defrosted.

"Welcome in!" a barista called from behind the register.

After sliding the door shut behind me, I ordered myself a cappuccino.

Fire Roasters was ridiculously packed even after 5:00 in the evening. Students typed on their laptops, children giggled at each other's whipped cream mustaches, and starry-eyed adults chatted during coffee dates. The many noises merged together into a soft, comforting hum.

I stared at my favorite spot. The two-seat table in front of the brick fireplace was arguably the most uncomfortable location in Fire Roasters. Any normal person wouldn't choose to sit within an arm's reach from a fire in such a hot room, but the table's low desirability meant that it was always empty—even on busy days—and I liked being able to call it *my spot*.

The barista slid my cappuccino onto the counter, and I grabbed the warm paper cup before heading to my table.

I hadn't gone to school since Wednesday, so I scanned the surrounding faces for any guys from Damon. The last thing I wanted to deal with was answering questions about my absence or my memory loss.

Once I knew the coast was clear, I set my cup on the walnut table, grabbed my phone from the pocket of my jeans, and took a seat.

*Dr. Singh, where are you?* I took a quick sip of my foamy cappuccino before searching for her phone number online. *There you are.*

I held my thumb over the call button, but the fireplace to my right distracted me. The heat from the flames left the right half of my face significantly hotter than my left, so I walked around the table and sat on the other side, giving my left cheek a chance to catch up in warmth.

*Stop stalling.*

I forced my thumb against the screen and raised the ringing phone to my ear.

"Hello?" Dr. Singh's groggy voice proved that she hadn't reached any kind of scientific breakthrough since we'd last spoken.

"Hi," I said. "This is Isaiah Sargo. We met on Wednesday."

"Isaiah!" Dr. Singh's voice softened. "How are you?"

"I have a question for you, actually. If you don't mind."

"You want the money back, don't you?"

"What?"

"The money you dropped off earlier today?"

I pursed my lips. *Classic Isaiah.* Of course he'd return the money we'd earned under the assumption that I didn't remember our scam. And with this new persona I had to play, there was nothing I could do to convince him to get the money back. All that time we'd spent in Dr. Singh's office was wasted. All my—

She cleared her throat. "Is something wrong?"

"Well, yeah. Yeah, something is. And it's not about the money." Now my left cheek was getting too hot, but I rolled my eyes at the thought of moving to the other side again. It was like my brain wanted me to be an idiot by default. "You see, I—I just—I've been having a really hard time dealing with Jeremy's memory loss. I was wondering if there was any way to—you know..."

I trailed off as a girl sat at the small table next to mine, my shoulders relaxing as I noticed that her earbuds were in. I lowered my voice anyway —just in case—and finished my statement.

"I was wondering if there was a way you could get me to lose my memories too."

Silence.

"Hello?" I muttered.

Dr. Singh sighed from the other end of the line. "Oh, Isaiah." I could hear her ruffling through papers, not even invested in our conversation anymore. "Jeremy needs you right now. You know that."

I sipped my cappuccino as Dr. Singh lectured me on how important it was to live through with my memories. I was my brother's lifeguard, his living diary—and other nonsense like that.

"But," I said slowly, "if I *were* to go through with it, what would that entail? Some kind of hypnotic? Old-school lobotomy? On a scale of one to ten, how painful should I expect it to be?"

"Please, stop with the nonsense. No one knows what caused this yet, so how could we possibly replicate it? If we had a way to perform such a massive memory-erasure safely and effectively, we'd likely know of a way to reverse it. So I'm sorry, but that's not an option."

The once-sweet coffee now left a bitter taste in my mouth.

Although I'd known this result could be a possibility, it still stung to hear Dr. Singh's words.

I had thought that I'd only had two options—I could either keep up this act and live with the constant worry of getting caught gnawing at the back of my head like a parasite, or I could come clean and submit the rage of my parents. But then I remembered Dr. Singh, my light at the end of the tunnel. This new Jeremy—this persona I'd been playing—perhaps I could truly become him.

But apparently the light at the end of the tunnel was nothing more than a flashlight. There was hope that I'd someday be able to go through a memory-erasure procedure, but now that depended on drastic medical advancements regarding Remembrance Week, and it was likely the battery in my flashlight would die before then.

"Alright, I'll make you a deal." Dr. Singh broke the silence, reminding me that I was even on a call with her in the first place. "If through my research I discover a way of performing such a procedure safely, you'll be the first to know."

Her words were nothing more than candy for a crying toddler. A way to cheer me up without addressing the root problem. Even if she were to discover a method, the scientific community would likely consider removing memories unethical, and arranging to do so could lead to serious legal issues. Dr. Singh would never go through the trouble for me, even if it were possible.

*Who am I kidding?* I took another bitter sip of my cappuccino. *The flashlight was already dead when I found it.*

"Thanks, Dr. Singh."

"You're welcome, Isaiah."

A beep marked the end of our call, as well as the end to my hope for a way out of this nightmare. I pulled the phone away from my ear, tossed the device onto the table, and downed the last few drops of coffee from my paper cup.

Ever since Rei moved away, I'd felt nothing but lost.

But now all I felt was *trapped*.

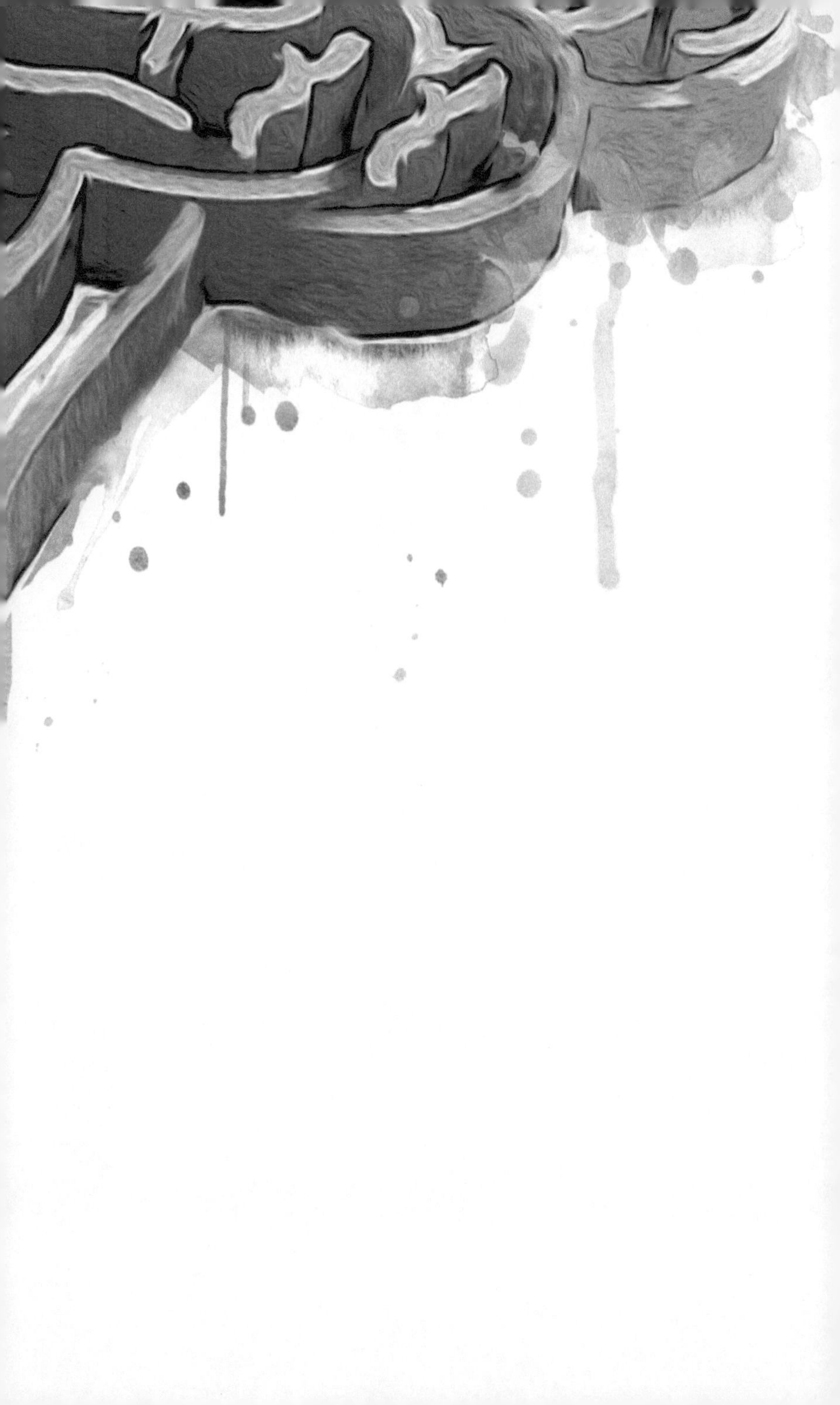

# ari

*Where did you learn this, Ari?*

I pulled both ends of a bobby pin away from each other to form a ninety-degree angle. After scraping the rubber piece off the straight end of the bobby pin with my fingernails, I pinched the now-sharp tip into a slight curve.

*You've definitely done this before.*

My parents had left me home alone for the first time since I'd woken up, and I used the opportunity to break into the mysterious room they'd been steering me away from. I didn't care whether I was being paranoid or if they actually had something to hide, but I knew that only the truth could bring me peace.

I reached into the front pocket of my khaki pants for a second bobby pin, which I modified into a lever by folding the curved end.

My fingers moved on their own as I jammed both bobby pins into the keyhole and fiddled with the pieces. After a few trials, the door swung open with a satisfying *pop*, revealing what my mother had referred to as a messy storage room.

*Except this isn't a messy storage room.*

The space looked as though it'd been lived in yesterday. Sheets and quilts of different shades of blue covered the unmade bed in the corner of the room, and heavy drapes hung over both windows, blocking out any natural light. I flicked the light switch on to get a clearer view before stepping inside and shutting the door behind me.

I tucked the bobby pins into my pocket. To my left was an arrangement of framed family photos stacked into piles. I recognized myself and my parents, but one unfamiliar face sent a chill down my spine. The young man had dark brown curls that matched my own, my mother's honey-colored eyes, and a smile even more charming than my father's. In some of the photos, he stood next to me, often with his arm around my shoulder.

*I'm sorry*, I thought as I pried my eyes from the nameless face, making my way toward a desk between the two curtained windows. *I don't remember you.*

My tan socks looked dull in comparison to the cool-toned paint stains that decorated the cream carpet in unintentional patterns. But although the stains intrigued me, the sketches sitting on the wooden desk completely knocked my breath away.

The drawings were nearly identical to the photos I'd seen of the *Seahorse* painting online.

Ever since I'd received that letter, M.L.C. had been nothing but a mystery to me. At times it almost felt as though the artist had shown up out of thin air to create one piece before vanishing to where they'd come from. Yet here I was, standing in a room of my very own home with sketches of what looked like early concepts of the same painting.

At the edge of the desk was a black notebook, its cover splattered with blue paint stains, just like the carpet. I wrapped my fingers around the front and back covers and flipped through endless pages of cursive handwriting. Near the beginning of the notebook I found a nearly blank page, nothing written apart from the name *Miles Cortez*.

*M.L.C.* I dropped the notebook onto the desk and reached for my seahorse pendant. *Miles L. Cortez.*

The dead artist whose painting I'd been encouraged to steal.

After taking a seat in Miles's desk and reading some of his journal entries, I discovered a few key facts about him. One, he had been my older brother of six years and would spend a lot of time with the old Ari—my name popped up a lot. Two, he had been in a horrible bike accident about two years ago that had severely impacted his mental health. And three, he had loved painting more than anything.

*"Some believe certain people, experiences, or objects might help bring back lost memories,"* my father had explained.

If the key to reviving old memories wasn't to eat sweet lemon chicken, perhaps the key was to steal my brother's painting. *Seahorse* must have been important to the old Ari, potentially important enough to bring her memories back—just as the anonymous letter had claimed, and just as the latest research had supported.

I rushed from Miles's room and into my own, grabbing a hooded corduroy jacket and a ten-dollar bill on my way out of the house.

There was no chance I could break into the Pentaware Art Museum without visiting it first. The pictures I'd found online only showed what the front of the building looked like—which I'd already seen on my recurring walks with Stella last week—and the exterior told me nothing about the museum's security. Were there cameras inside? Motion sensors? Alarms?

I lost myself in my buzzing head on the way to the museum, my feet moving on their own as though the route were ingrained in my muscle memory. Perhaps it was.

By the time I reached a sidewalk lined with white oak trees to my right, I woke from my daze to catch glimpses of the museum between clumps of red leaves. My heart pounded with the anticipation of seeing my brother's painting in person.

A few droplets of rain landed on my head. I flipped over the hood of my jacket and jogged down the sidewalk, the evil rain matching my pace. My goal was to reach the museum before getting drenched, but as I followed the sidewalk around the corner and approached the front steps to the building, I forgot about the rain and came to a complete stop.

*How beautiful.*

The towering stone building nearly convinced me that I'd traveled back in time. A tall row of steps led to its grand entrance, where four gothic pillars supported the roof overhang. Between the middle two pillars was a pair of paneled ebony doors with golden handles.

At this point the rain was literally streaming over my eyes and blinding me, so I shook my fascination away and headed up the lengthy rows of steps.

My clothes were soaked by the time I walked under the roof overhang. I rubbed my arms, scraping a layer of water off my skin as I approached a booth by the front doors. It was nothing more than a closet-sized stone box with a circular cutout for the employee inside to converse with museum visitors. Like a movie theater pay stand—but upgraded.

I dug through the right pocket of my jacket for the ten dollars I'd brought with me. The bill was soggy, which was a bit embarrassing—but it'd get me into the museum, and that's what mattered most. I pinched the money, trying to squeeze out as much water as possible before raising my chin to face the employee inside.

My eyes widened as I mistook the boy in the booth as Jeremy Sargo from my memory counseling discussion group yesterday afternoon. I wouldn't find out until the following day that the boy working at the museum was actually Isaiah, Jeremy's twin brother.

He wore a forest-green hoodie with a golden bird-head logo embroidered into the fabric at the chest. After a few blinks, I recognized the symbol from Damon Academy, the all-boys school Stella had pointed out to me during one of our walks together.

The boy I thought was Jeremy flipped a page of his textbook, which rested on a narrow wooden platform next to a cash register. When he didn't acknowledge my presence, I cleared my throat and stuck the ten-dollar bill through the booth cutout.

"Sorry," he muttered. "I didn't hear you."

Jeremy took the money without looking at me, his eyes still trailing over the textbook page.

*Stella was right—Damon Academy students really do take school seriously.*
"One adult?"

I nodded as he raised his chin to face me.

When our eyes met, Jeremy froze. It almost looked as though he were about to smile, but the light indication of warmth faded almost instantly, his brows knitting into a frown.

"Back to work already?" I asked, genuinely curious. The fact that Jeremy had jumped back into his job so soon after losing his memories was both impressive and a little odd. "I'm surprised you've managed to memorize the rules again so fast. Or did you already know them? I guess rules are part of semantic memories, aren't they?"

"What rules? Semantic?" Jeremy held his head still for a few seconds before shaking it lightly, his eyes drifting to the ten-dollar bill in his hands. "Is this some kind of joke?" He stuck the money through the cutout, refusing my purchase.

I wrapped my jacket around myself tighter, shivering as the wind slipped under my damp hair. I was waiting for him to explain himself, but when I didn't take the money back, he flicked the bill in my direction.

The bill fluttered in front of me and landed on the stone floor.

"Sorry," Jeremy said, voice shaky. "We're closed."

I leaned over and retrieved the ten dollars resting by my soggy sneakers. After skeptically stashing the money into my pocket, I glanced at a golden sign above the two ebony doors, which clearly stated that the museum closed at 5:00 on Sunday evenings, nearly two hours from now.

I tried to catch Jeremy's eyes, but they continued to fly out of view.

"But—"

"Just stop, Ari." He flipped to another page of his textbook, and I could tell by how rapidly his eyes moved that he wasn't reading a word from it. "I just—I can't deal with this again."

I was about to ask Jeremy what *this* in his question had referred to, but I stiffened my jaw, stopping myself. The topic obviously made him uncomfortable, and although I was curious, I knew how annoying it was for people to pry about the past. He didn't seem like he was in the mood to talk, and as a fellow memory loss victim, I had to respect that.

"Okay." I took a deep breath and crossed my arms, pretending as though I knew exactly what he meant. "Thanks anyway."

It wasn't until later that night, as I lay in my bed staring at the ceiling, when I really started to second-guess my decision to leave Jeremy at the booth without pressing for a deeper explanation.

*"I just—I can't deal with this again."*

The boy I thought was Jeremy had made it seem as though I'd done something in the past, but we'd only met yesterday. Why had he given me the money back? It was like he didn't want me inside the museum, but why would that be? Did he know something about the letter? Did he know something about Miles?

The facts weren't lining up. The strong-minded Jeremy I'd met at the admissions booth was completely different from the Jeremy who'd been a nervous wreck at our meeting the day before.

If I wanted even a slim chance of getting my memories back, I needed to get into that museum. To let Jeremy's words stop me would be ridiculous, but maybe today's encounter had been a blessing in disguise. Jeremy obviously knew something, and that something might help me figure out why I'd been given a second chance and how I could redeem it successfully.

*Steal the painting during the next full moon,* the anonymous letter had read, *and your memories will return as soon as you leave the building.*

The next full moon was this Friday, five days from now.

I couldn't risk waiting around until Tuesday to ask Jeremy for answers at the next counseling meeting. With how nervous he'd been yesterday, and how bothered he'd been to see me at the museum, there was a chance he might not even show. I didn't know where he lived or anything about his work schedule either.

*Which leaves Plan C.*

My brain flashed with the logo embroidered into his hoodie.

*Damon Academy.*

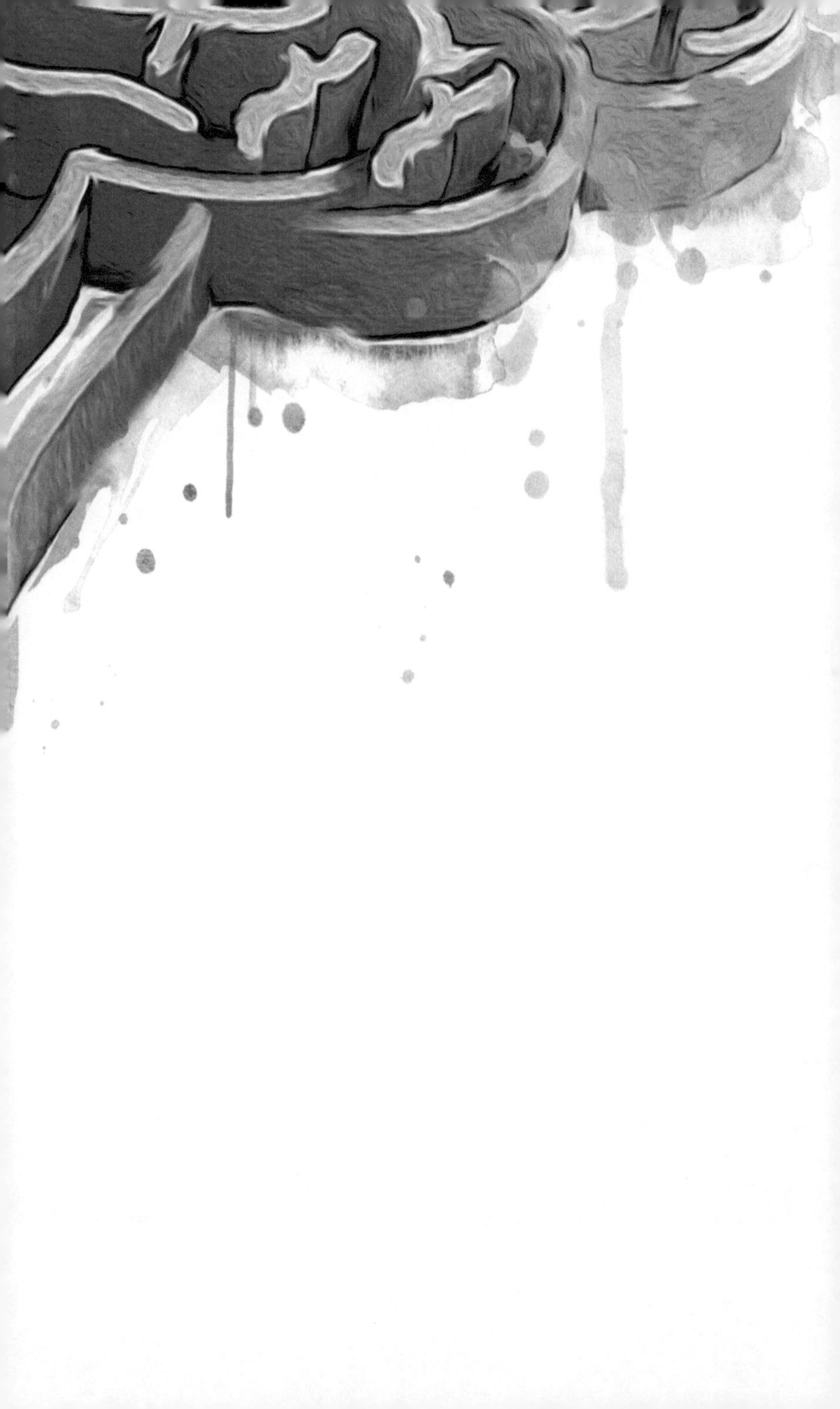

# c h a p t e r  6
# j e r e m y

"Jeremy?"

The woman's muffled voice did nothing to bring me back to my senses. I used my arms as pillows on my desk, nestling my head deeper into the depths of my blazer sleeves as the classroom filled with whispers.

*Maybe if I keep sleeping, they'll leave me alone.*

I'd spent the first four hours at Damon Academy with my pathetic head resting in my arms, and that hadn't been my own choice. My body was literally shutting down. I couldn't remember the last time I'd indulged in a full night's rest or a healthy plate of food. At this point I didn't care anymore.

"Jeremy?" the voice repeated. I finally made the connection that the woman calling my name was our school secretary, Priscilla.

The whispering came to a blunt halt as I pulled my head away from my cozy arms. Every guy had their eyes on me, peering over their shoulders at the back of the room, where I sat at the desk farthest from the classroom door.

Today was my first day at Damon since I'd pretended to lose my memories, and my peers now saw me as some jokester Remembrance Week had transformed into a delicate, confused teenage boy.

*In their eyes, am I even Jeremy anymore?*

I glanced at the back of my brother's head in the front row. Isaiah was the only person in the room who wasn't staring me down. Instead, he studied the history textbook in front of him, probably stressing over another exam. He'd always sucked at history.

"Good morning, Jeremy," Priscilla said in a sassy tone, bringing my attention to her presence in the doorway. Her playful grin hardly lasted more than a second, disappearing as she reminded herself that I'd lost my memories. "Your cousin's waiting for you in the lobby."

Isaiah looked up from his textbook. "Should I come too?"

Priscilla shrugged. "Up to you."

She may as well have said, *You think I care?*

Isaiah finally looked over his shoulder, his narrowed eyes landing on me. My stomach churned at the idea that he'd somehow figured me out, but he eventually returned to reading his textbook. I sighed softly and stood from my desk.

*Cousin, huh?* I had a lot of those, but they all lived outside of Oregon. I couldn't remember the last time I'd talked to one of them.

I tucked my hands into the pockets of my blazer as I walked down the aisle, trying to stop myself from awkwardly fidgeting with my fingers as I ignored the endless eyes following me from all directions.

Priscilla held the classroom door open, and my shoulders loosened as I entered the hall, finally escaping the pressure of being studied like some kind of exotic bird.

I waited for Priscilla to scold me or make an annoyed remark, but for the first time in history, we walked down the hallway together in complete silence.

Whenever Rei and I would get away with another scheme, the secretary would always catch on. Priscilla would pull us aside throughout the day, threatening us to get our acts together—but we never did, and she never followed through with telling our families what we'd done.

I smiled grimly at a memory from earlier this school year, when Rei and

I had covered her office desk with the creepy fan fiction we'd found her writing online. Priscilla had done nothing but lecture us personally, struggling to conceal her laughter the entire time. Despite playing the role of enemies, we brought a bit more fun to each other's routines here at Damon.

*But now I'm not supposed to remember any of it.*

"You don't have to be here, you know," Priscilla said in a much softer tone than usual. "If you need more time away from school, just let me know, and I'll get you a pass."

Priscilla would never dare show this empathetic side of herself to the old Jeremy, and although I was honored to know she cared this much about me despite all the trouble I'd caused, it felt wrong to learn how she felt in such a dishonest circumstance.

"If only this were another one of your pranks." Her deep green eyes turned hollow, and I realized that she was talking to the old Jeremy now, not to me. I was nothing but a corpse to share her parting goodbyes with. "I'm sorry, I just…"

Priscilla shook her head, stopping herself from saying more. And as we neared the end of the hall—which led into the lobby—the urge to come clean struck me harder than ever before. My family would never forgive me for lying about my memories, but Priscilla had always tolerated my mischief. Surely she'd understand.

*It* is *a prank*, I wanted to say. *Please, help me fix this!*

I bit my lip as we reached the end of the hallway and entered the bright lobby. My fingers folded into fists as I finally gathered the courage to tell her.

"Priscilla, I—"

But when my eyes landed on the person waiting for me, my confession trapped itself inside my throat.

The short-haired girl was not one of my cousins, but Ari Cortez—the memory counseling member who'd been placed in my discussion group the day before yesterday. She stood in the middle of the lobby with her arms crossed, eyes wandering to the glass display of sports trophies, the clothing racks of uniforms for sale, and the wall covered in class photos dating back to eighty years ago. The Damon Academy lobby truly was the definition of *school spirit.*

"Yes?" Priscilla asked. "What's wrong?"

"Uh—sorry. It's nothing."

"Well, alright then," she said to my back as I stepped forward into the lobby. "But remember—if you need more time, just talk to me."

I gritted my teeth as Priscilla traveled back the way we'd come, her heels clicking against the hallway floor. I could hardly believe that I'd nearly spilled my secret to her.

*How could I have been so sloppy, so impulsive, so—*

"It's even nicer on the inside." Ari peeled her eyes from the chandelier that hung from the lofty ceiling above us, her gaze landing on me as I approached her. "I might have to transfer."

I raised my brows, not expecting to hear a joke from the girl who hadn't smiled once during our first counseling meeting.

"I'm told we're known for having a nice campus," I said.

She took a seat on the nearest emerald-green sofa, and I sat on the opposite end of it, leaving a rather awkward gap of space between us.

While Ari stared down our lobby in awe, I frantically adjusted my disheveled tie and collar. I'd shown up to school looking like a mess, and maybe I'm oversharing at this point, but I couldn't remember the last time I'd showered either.

"Is it your first day too?" Ari asked.

I nodded.

"Not much fun, is it?"

"No." I paused to yawn. "Not at all."

Ever since my failed talk with Dr. Singh on Saturday, I'd felt nothing but numb. Stuck. Trapped in a life I had no interest in. But Ari's strange appearance intrigued me that Monday, and it was nice to be intrigued by something again.

"Don't you go to Pentaware High?" I asked.

"It's lunch break." Ari eyed my uniform, which I'd grown used to people doing at this point.

"But Pentaware has a closed campus policy," I said, drawing her eyes back to my face, "so technically, you're not supposed to leave, even during lunch."

Ari shrugged, and I felt a twinge in the corner of my lips—a subtle urge to grin. Based on my first impression of her, I'd assumed she was the type to take all rules seriously, no matter how harmless breaking them could be.

*But how does she know I go to Damon?* I hadn't worn my uniform to the counseling meeting on Saturday, and I couldn't recall mentioning my school's name.

"Look," she said, "I need to get into that museum."

"Museum? What museum?"

"The only museum in town," Ari stated as though it were obvious. "The Pentaware Art Museum."

"Right." I couldn't tell where she was going with this. "And?"

"What do you mean *and*?" She leaned toward me, shortening the distance between us. "How am I supposed to get inside when you won't let me buy a ticket?"

The clicking of the analog clock on the wall filled the air until the realization left me gasping.

"Oh! You must mean my brother Isaiah. He works there part-time."

"Identical twins. So that's it." Ari nodded to herself, making a mental note. "Did Isaiah lose his memories too?"

"No." I'd responded way too quickly, so I pinched the skin on the back of my hand to remind myself to stay calm. "It's uh—it's just me who lost them."

"Do you have any idea why he wouldn't let me buy a ticket yesterday?"

I shook my head, finding it hard to picture Isaiah denying entry to anyone at the museum. According to him, not many people showed up, and he was usually bored out of his mind at that booth. With his strange passion for *sharing art with the masses*, I would have thought he'd let anyone inside who displayed even the slightest hint of interest.

But what confused me even more was why Ari was so fixated on getting into that museum in the first place.

"You know, us memory loss victims care a lot about the past. Surely there's something in the museum that meant a lot to you." My frown deepened as she turned her face away from me. "What are you searching for?"

"I'm not sure what you mean."

*What a rookie.* Apparently she couldn't make eye contact and lie at the same time.

"Nevermind." Ari stood from the sofa and took a few steps toward the front door. "I'm sorry for wasting your time."

"No!" I sprung to my feet, my voice so loud it made both of us flinch. "Really, you're not wasting my time. Let me help."

I could hardly believe the desperateness in my voice. I'd spoken as though my life depended on it, but at the time, it really felt like it. My life was spiraling out of control, and I had no clue what to do with myself anymore. I was slowly turning into the shell of a person the other memory loss victims had become, but unlike them, I knew what I'd lost.

And it pained me.

*What's wrong with my head?* I asked myself as Ari looked over her shoulder with narrowed eyes. *Why am I doing this?*

Perhaps all I needed was a new project to work on. One last plan to keep me occupied. It didn't even matter what it was at this point. I just needed a distraction.

"You'll help me get into the museum?"

"Of course I will."

"What if it's not for a good reason?" Ari gave the door a final glance before turning to face me. "What if, theoretically, it's for something illegal?"

"Doesn't matter if it's theoretical or not." I smiled, and for the first time in a while, I felt alive again. "I'm in."

Ari crossed her arms. "And what's in it for you?"

"According to my classmates, I was a bit of a troublemaker." My voice was more solemn than I'd expected it to be, and I internally applauded myself for that. "But ever since I woke up, I haven't done anything the old Jeremy would've done. Maybe getting involved in some kind of scheme will help me understand who I used to be."

A perfect lie—vulnerable and all.

"I get it. That's why I'm doing this too." Ari scanned the room, ensuring it was still empty before landing the final blow. "I'm stealing a painting this Friday."

"Sounds fun. So what's the plan?"

Ari blinked.

"You have a plan, right?"

"I'm working on it," she said in a strained voice, reaching for her necklace like she had during our counseling meeting.

"Does your necklace have something to do with that painting?"

"Maybe."

The bell rang to mark the start of Damon's lunch break, but we both ignored it.

Ari dropped her pendant. "But that's not important. What I really need to figure out is how secure the building is. Where the cameras are located, if there's an alarm system, how many windows there are—those kinds of things. My parents don't let me roam alone too much, and I'm still confused about your brother and how—"

"Yeah, yeah. Understood. I'll head to the museum for you after school."

"Really? You will?"

I nodded.

"Wow. Uh—thanks, Jeremy." Ari's face brightened. "Draw a floor plan of the building. I mean, if you can."

I wasn't sure whether to be impressed by her level of dedication, or annoyed that she thought I was incapable of drawing a floor plan. Damon was the only high school in the area that even offered an architecture elective.

"Floor plan," I repeated in a monotone voice. "Got it."

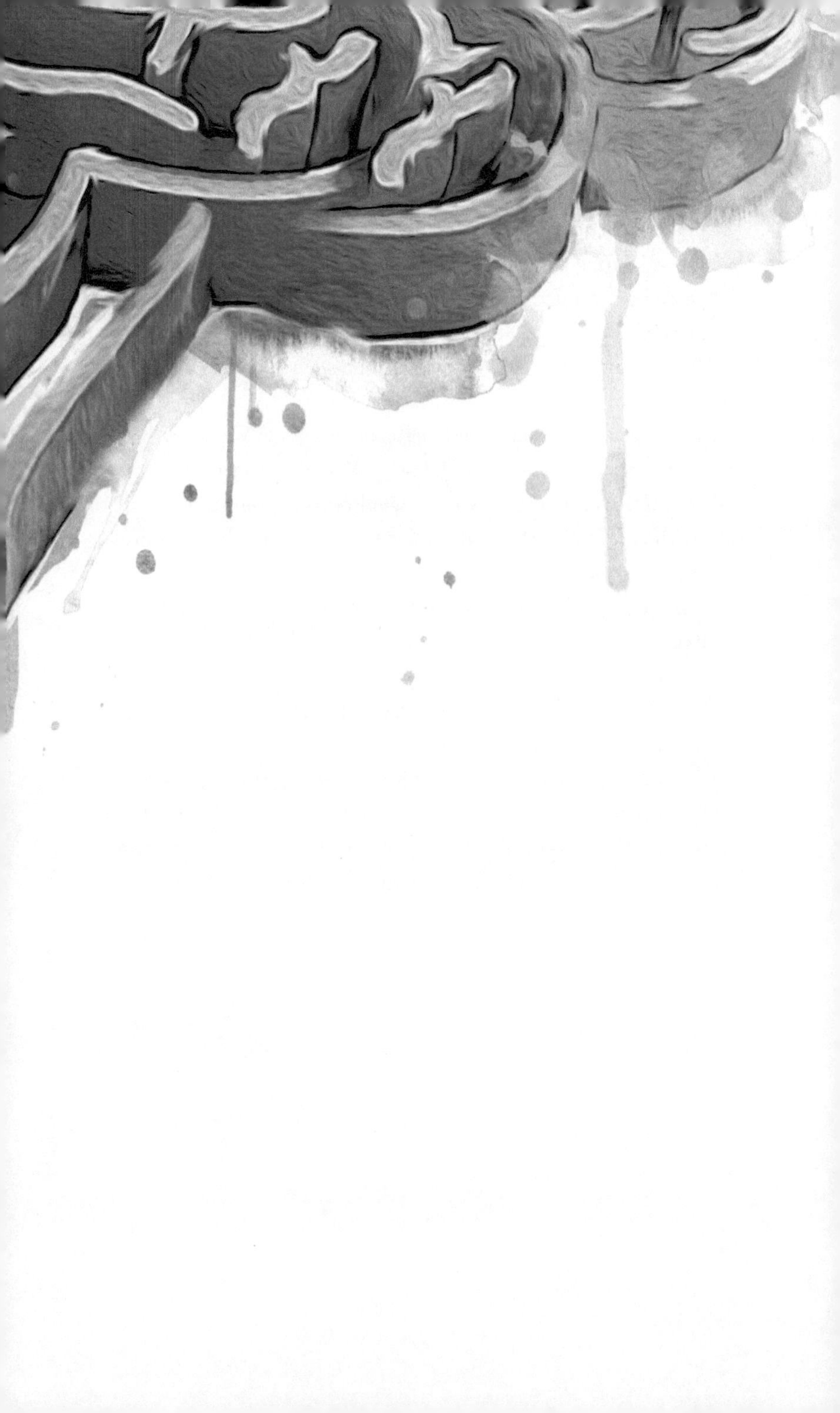

c h a p t e r  7

# a r i

"Five minutes left. Why don't we talk about school?" Emmett's animated voice stuck out like a sore thumb in the dreary gymnasium atmosphere. "For those of you who started your first day this week, how did it go?"

Piper and Jeremy turned in my direction, urging me to speak first, but my mind went blank. *How did it go?* Emmett could not have possibly come up with a more loaded question.

Stella had shown me around yesterday morning before school, just like she'd promised my begging mother to. During our walk around campus, she'd told me that students had been panicked out of their minds last week.

*"It was an absolute madhouse in here. Nearly half the school didn't even show, and those who did were extremely paranoid,"* Stella shared while leading me to my first class. *"I'm so glad Remembrance Week has been confirmed as nothing but a short biological anomaly. Things are finally getting back to normal."*

But Stella had been wrong. The fear still lived on at Pentaware High School. It had simply taken a different form.

Heads would turn as I'd walk down the hall. Students would whisper during class with their pupils pointed in my direction. Teachers would kneel by the side of my desk to check in on my emotional state. As one of the few memory loss victims who had shown up to Pentaware High School this week, I attracted attention no matter where I hid, but no one dared to ask me the questions I knew were buzzing through their minds. Perhaps they didn't want me to feel uncomfortable, but all they managed to accomplish was make me feel like even more of a stranger than I already was.

Some articles reported that memory loss victims had been gifted with the ability to retain new information faster—that our minds were like a sponge, soaking everything in as though we were babies again—but I found that theory hard to get on board with. Locker combinations, where my classes were located, my teachers' names, which desks I usually sat in—all of it was new to me, and I found myself jumbling everything together until I was sitting in the wrong desks, attempting to open the wrong lockers, and showing up to nearly every class late with sweat on my forehead and labored breaths.

I cleared my throat, breaking my lengthy trail of thought.

"Monday was fine," I said.

"Yeah?" Jeremy shrugged. "Same here."

We both turned to Piper, who already had a growing smile on her face.

"Well," Piper said, "I'm homeschooled, so it's been an easy transition."

"I'm sure it has," Jeremy said. His statement had come across as a bit rude, but I didn't blame him. Piper was quite the talker, and he likely wanted to keep her from spouting off into one of her tangents again.

*"I'm fourteen, and a fun fact is that my room is filled with crime novels. Practically made of them."* My eyes widened as I remembered Piper's introduction during our last meeting. *"It almost looks like I was planning something myself."*

"Piper?"

"Yeah?"

"On Saturday you told us that your room's filled with crime novels." I forced myself to speak at a faster pace to imitate genuine interest. "Have you read any of them yet?"

I knew it was wrong to take advantage of Piper for my own benefit, but getting my memories back was all that mattered at this point, and I was willing to do whatever it'd take—as long as it meant getting away with the act unscathed.

Piper's jaw dropped. "Are you kidding? Oh, I've read tons! I'm dedicated to getting through my entire collection before the end of next year." She gazed at the ceiling as she recalled a recent memory. "You know what's funny? In one of my diary entries, the old me wrote that I wished I could wipe my memories and reread my favorite books for the first time again. Looks like Remembrance Week granted Piper her greatest wish."

I waited, debating whether or not to ask another question—but then I remembered how I'd regretted not asking Jeremy's brother any follow-up questions when he'd denied me an admissions ticket on Sunday, so I shut down my overcomplicated brain and asked Piper if she'd read about any heists.

Piper opened her mouth, but Jeremy interrupted her with a sudden burst of laughter, his back bending over into hysteria. My face grew hot at the realization that he was making fun of me for using Piper to gather information.

Thankfully, Piper ignored him and dived into what she'd been dying to tell me only seconds prior.

"I've read about all kinds of heists. Bank heists, museum heists, school heists—"

"Museum heists?" I asked.

Jeremy wiped the sides of his eyes, finally catching his breath.

"Museum heists are my absolute favorite! Have you ever heard of the term *artnapping*?" Piper pushed her curls behind her shoulders. "Sounds way cooler than *stealing a painting*, right?"

Jeremy pursed his lips—his smile gone—and I got the impression that he was impressed Piper might be a helpful resource after all.

"So," Jeremy added, "how's it done?"

As Piper jumped into an explanation about the artnapping stories she'd read so far, Jeremy winked in my direction.

*Really?* I rolled my eyes. *I was the one who asked about her books in the first place.*

"In one of the novels I read," Piper said, "the protagonist digs a tunnel that runs under the museum."

I imagined myself with a shovel outside the Pentaware Art Museum, hopelessly digging into the dirt.

*I'll pass on that one.*

"And in this other book, a group of three dress up like the museum staff to blend in."

Isaiah had been wearing a Damon Academy school hoodie in the admissions booth, which likely meant the museum didn't have staff uniforms we could match to blend in.

*Another pass.*

"But in reality," Piper said, her voice finally slowing down, "most art theft in real life occurs through simple smash-and-grabs, or hiding out in a closet until closing time—that kind of thing. Books tend to hyper-glamorize."

*Simple smash-and-grabs?*

I figured the phrase likely meant breaking through a window, grabbing the target, and leaving. Seemed easy enough.

Emmett clapped his hands from the middle of the room.

"Great work, everyone." He spun in circles, making eye contact with all three groups spread across the gymnasium. "I'll see you this Saturday."

Jeremy caught my eye with a quick nod before heading for the door. We had plans to discuss the heist after today's meeting, and honestly, I was looking forward to it. Until yesterday I'd been convinced that I'd have to go through this alone, but now I had someone to help me out, and that made the task far less daunting.

I took a step toward the door, on my way to follow Jeremy out.

"Ari?"

I glanced over my shoulder, half-expecting Piper to tell me a long-winded story she'd read in one of her diary entries, but instead, she asked me a question.

"Don't you think something's off about Jeremy?"

I crossed my arms and turned to fully face her. "Why would you think that?"

"For real? You haven't noticed?" Piper asked in a mocking tone. She stepped forward, yanking at the loose fabric of my jacket sleeve as though that'd somehow help me understand where she was coming from. Her voice rose a few pitches as the enthusiasm completely engulfed her. "At our last meeting, Jeremy was a mess, but today he's been all calm and confident. He even burst into laughter when you asked about my novels. It's almost like he—like he—"

"Like he what?" I gently wiggled my sleeve out of her grip.

Piper leaned forward and whispered, "It's like he got his memories back."

I froze, my head replaying Jeremy's nervous behavior from our first meeting three days ago. Yes, Piper was right about how he'd changed, but that was our *first meeting*. We were all a bit more stiff than we were today.

I reminded myself that Piper had likely stayed up all night reading those crime novels she was committed to finishing. I couldn't let her fictional tales drip into my reality.

"Don't worry about it, okay?" I offered a quick smile before walking away from her, grabbing my backpack from the clump of belongings by the door, and leaving the gymnasium.

*It's time for business.*

I rushed down the hallway, passing a few chatting counseling group members on my way out. Thanks to school and this meeting, I hadn't had any time today to plan for the break-in, and I was itching to get started.

Jeremy stood waiting for me at the bottom of the front steps. We made a sharp right turn around the corner of Pentaware High School, our feet leaving the sturdy concrete of the entrance and landing on the gravel courtyard that ran along the side of the building. The shady trees and the vast array of picnic tables made the courtyard a hot spot on campus during school hours, and it felt eerie to see it this empty.

"So I saw that painting you were talking about. It's on the second floor." Jeremy ran his fingers along the brick wall of the building, taking dramatically slow steps. "But I don't get it. Why would you wanna steal a painting of some horse-fish hybrid?"

"I think it's pretty. That's all." My answer was instantaneous because I'd prepared it the night before, knowing he'd ask eventually. "And it's a sea-horse, not a horse-fish. In Greek it's called a *hippocampus*, and the crea-ture symbolizes hope."

"So you're telling me that a part of the brain is named after a horse-fish?"

"*Sea-horse*," I corrected for the second time. "But yes. I guess so."

We sat across from each other at the nearest picnic table, and Jeremy filled me in on the information he'd managed to squeeze out of one of the museum employees yesterday afternoon.

"Obviously I couldn't ask too many questions or she'd get suspicious," he said. "But according to her, security's pretty weak. She's trying to convince her manager to add an alarm system, especially after some attempted theft a few months ago."

My phone buzzed on the picnic table, Stella's face filling the screen. The old Ari had chosen a rather embarrassing contact photo—her face twisted into a wrinkly, disgusted expression. But once again, that plaid jacket was the same.

Jeremy pointed at the screen. "Stella Pierce?"

I grabbed my phone and declined the call. I'd been avoiding Stella all day, but it was for her own sake. She wanted to spend time with the old Ari, not the new one. It would be in both of our best interests for me to direct my complete focus into succeeding this Friday.

"Before Remembrance Week, she was my best friend," I said in a boring tone, hoping he'd lose interest. "I'll call her back later, but right now I need to focus on getting that painting."

Jeremy pursed his lips, and I could tell he had a million questions but wasn't sure where to begin. He eventually held his hand out and said, "Let me give you my number."

"Huh?"

"For communication? We're a team now, aren't we?"

He'd made a fair point, so I handed him my phone, and he started typing his number into a new contact. I stifled a laugh as he took a selfie for his contact photo, contorting his face into a disgusted look that rivaled Stella's. He gave my phone back with a grin.

I was going to comment on the photo he'd taken, but by the time I looked up from the screen again, Jeremy had moved on to unzipping the backpack next to him.

"All this trouble just cause you think the painting's pretty? Did you really think I'd buy that?" He rustled through the many papers in the main compartment of his backpack, eyes narrowed. I sensed a hidden frustration in his voice. "Seriously, Ari. What are you doing this for?"

"Nothing." I set my phone on the picnic table before meeting his eyes with a blank face.

"You know, if you're gonna lie, you could at least try." He zipped his backpack shut, now with a paper in his hands. "I just really hope you're not doing this for the money. Trying to sell a stolen painting is one of the easiest ways to get caught for the crime. Ask any idiot art thief behind bars."

"Relax. I'm not doing it for the money."

"But if not for the money, then what for?"

"Maybe I'm just creating chaos to spend time with you," I said. "People don't think straight when they're in love."

"Good. That one was more convincing." Jeremy leaned forward with a smirk. "But you still didn't fool me."

I laughed, more in response to my own words than his.

*I didn't know you were a jokester, Ari.*

My humor dissipated as Jeremy set the paper from his backpack on the picnic table.

"You drew a floor plan?" I asked, observing his sketches. He'd split the page into four boxes, each section representing one story of the building.

"I told Isaiah I needed some time to myself after school yesterday and walked straight to the museum. All the employees thought I was him, and it took me forever to draw this thing out without them noticing. It was a living nightmare, so you better be grateful."

I took the paper into my own grip, my eyes widening at the familiar lines. The floor plan he'd drawn perfectly matched the ones I'd found in my room the day I'd woken up—the ones my mother had taken away.

"Of course I'm grateful." I folded the page and tucked it into the pocket of my jacket. "Thank you. It's nice to be around someone who knows what I'm going through."

My own words had shocked me at first, but when I analyzed them, I realized they were true. I thought of my parents, who had dedicated hours to showing me pictures of my old self and sharing stories about her. I thought of Stella, who had convinced me that she would help jog my memories because she knew the old Ari the best. I thought of the students and teachers who had watched me like a hawk, scared to ask questions in fear that my forgotten past was sensitive material. Even other memory loss victims like Piper were constantly talking about the new things they'd discovered about their old selves.

Ever since I'd woken up, Jeremy was the only person who wasn't living in the past. He didn't know me as the old Ari, but as me.

"Everyone sees me as someone I'm not." I gulped, hoping that his silence after everything I'd said didn't mean I was spouting nonsense. "And I'm worried I'll never be able to fix that, you know?"

"Yeah, I know." Jeremy looked away from me, his posture loosening. "Me too."

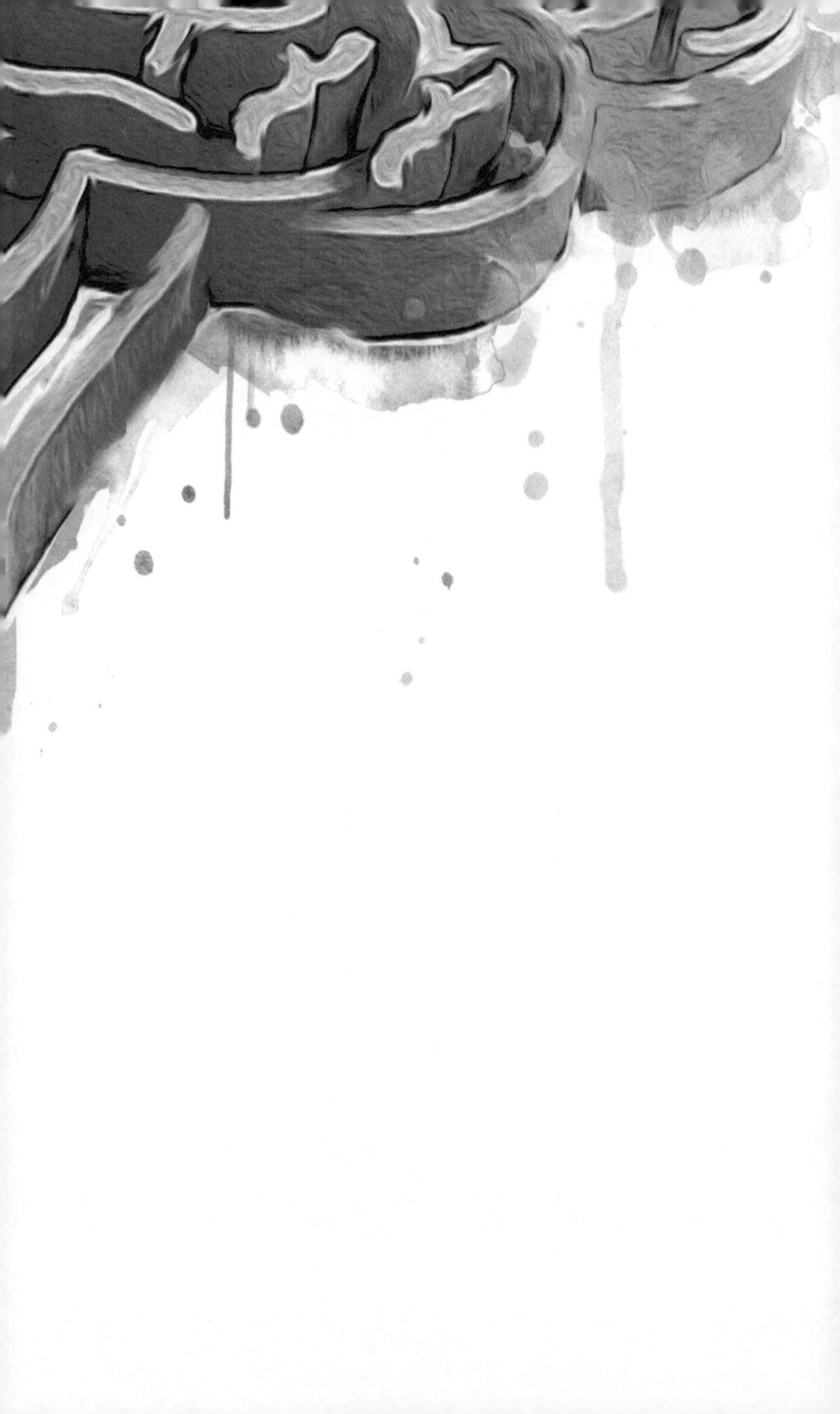

c h a p t e r   8

# j e r e m y

I sat on the front steps at midnight, three hours before our planned heist. I hadn't bothered to change out of my Damon Academy uniform, so I'd bundled myself up in a generic, black athletic jacket—the kind everyone owns—to cover up my collared shirt and tie in the security footage.

*"And it's a sea-horse, not a horse-fish,"* Ari had told me three days prior. *"In Greek it's called a* hippocampus, *and the creature symbolizes hope."*

The curiosity of why Ari was targeting *Seahorse* specifically hadn't struck me until Monday afternoon, when I'd stood on the second floor of the Pentaware Art Museum after school, staring at the oil painting by M.L.C. The artwork felt oddly familiar. I was positive I'd seen it somewhere, but I couldn't put my finger on where.

"A symbol of hope," I whispered, my brain flashing with the image of Ari reaching for her seahorse pendant, a habit of hers that remained unexplained. "Why did she mention that?"

When I'd first agreed to help Ari with her artnapping scheme, the reason why she wanted to break into the museum to steal a painting hadn't been a concern of mine. All I cared about was doing something the old Jeremy would have done. To be myself again, even if it would only last a few days.

Yet what overpowered my curiosity was a numbness I didn't understand the cause of until my eyes landed on the full moon in the sky.

*Tonight is the end of our story, isn't it?*

Ari and I had met at McCloud Park after school on Wednesday to go over our options for how we'd break in smoothly and cover our tracks. On Thursday we'd walked along the perimeter of the museum together to search for an ideal point of entry. And the more time I spent with Ari, the more I understood how much this painting meant to her. I'd gotten involved for my own selfish reasons, but it would be a lie to say that I didn't care whether or not she'd feel accomplished tonight.

If only her success didn't mean the end to the best distraction I'd found yet.

Over the past few days, I'd been happier than I'd ever been, but by sunrise I'd no longer have an excuse to spend time with Ari. She'd be nothing more than a girl in my memory counseling group, and I'd go back to being stuck in the guinea pig wheel I'd built for myself.

*Maybe I can tell her we need more time to plan—that we aren't ready yet.*

I wanted to postpone the heist for my own sake, but stealing *Seahorse* was all Ari wanted. Was it really right to purposefully delay such an important event?

The front door swung open, interrupting my moral dilemma.

I looked over my shoulder to spot Isaiah closing the door behind him. He'd changed out of his uniform and into a pair of jeans and a gray t-shirt, which was rather odd for him. Normally at this hour, he'd be wearing his pajama pants and brushing his teeth, preparing to end the day. It almost seemed as though he were ready to head out tonight himself.

"You okay?" he asked, walking over and taking a seat next to me on the porch step.

"I'm good." I turned my attention back to the starry night sky. My breath clouded my vision in the air as I muttered, "Just relaxing."

It felt wrong to chat with Isaiah casually again. Ever since I'd faked my memory loss last Thursday, the two of us had only grown further apart.

"I—uh—I got a strange call today."

"Oh yeah?" I exhaled another breath and watched the white cloud melt into the darkness. "From who?"

Isaiah rubbed his bare arms with the palms of his hands. Either the cold was reaching him too, or the words he was about to spout were too chilling to bear in such harsh weather.

"Dr. Singh."

My eyes jumped from star to star, scanning the sky for answers. "Who's that?"

"She asked if I was feeling better since I last called, which I found a little strange, considering how I never called her."

*"Can I get your number?"* Dr. Singh had asked my brother before we'd left her office last week. *"I'd like to be in touch in case I have any follow-up questions."*

On Saturday I'd called Dr. Singh at Fire Roasters from my own number, pretending to be Isaiah. She must have chosen to check on him by calling the number on her notepad rather than scrolling back through her list of recent calls.

*Sloppy.* I closed my eyes. *How could I have been so sloppy?*

"I'm a bit relieved, actually," my brother said after a moment of silence. "I'm glad we didn't lose you, but I'm disappointed that you never told us the truth. You know how hard this has been on Mom and Dad."

"No, you don't get it." My fiery voice sent him leaning away from me. "Don't you see what would happen if Mom and Dad found out? It'd be a complete mess, and you'd be dragged into it too."

"I have *always* been dragged into your problems." Isaiah was breathing heavier now, his rage finally seeping through. "Don't pretend like I'm the enemy here when you know what's right. Just stay home and forget about the museum tonight."

My strained face softened. "What?"

"Isn't that what you're planning? To break into the Pentaware Art Museum with Ari?"

"How could you possibly—"

"So I'm right?" Isaiah muttered softly, as though he were hoping his assumption had been wrong. "She lost her memories, didn't she? You must have met her in that counseling group."

"But how—how did you—"

"On Monday, after school. You went to the museum before my shift," he said, my eyes widening at his explanation. "You really thought my co-workers would pretend they hadn't seen me? They were continuing conversations I didn't remember starting. I mean, I was only a little confused back then, but Dr. Singh's call confirmed my suspicion."

It was obvious. Such a ridiculous slip-up, and I'd never stopped to give it a second thought.

"It's nice of you to help her," Isaiah said. "But you're not doing it the right way. That painting won't do any good. So please, let this whole museum shenanigan go."

I nearly ripped the jacket off my shoulders, my blood boiling. I knew I shouldn't have been mad at Isaiah, but I couldn't help it.

I couldn't help it, because part of me knew he was right.

"Do you really want me to pretend like you don't remember our childhood for the rest of our lives?" His eyes glowed like the ends of two match sticks in a cave, and although we shared the same face, I couldn't help but feel as though I were staring into the eyes of a stranger. "Do you really want everyone to think that you lost your memories that day?"

I shook my head. "Isaiah, I—"

"Dude, you never woke up!" He raised his voice at me, and I couldn't remember the last time he'd done that. "I promise, I'll help you get through this. But you have to come clean."

*No.* I stood from the porch, my fingers reaching into the pocket of my jacket and fumbling for the keys to our car. *I don't have time for this.*

There was no chance Isaiah would be willing to keep my lie a secret. With him on my case, our parents would find out soon enough, and they'd hate me for what I'd done.

"Jeremy!" Isaiah called as I ran toward the car.

I threw myself into the driver's seat and slammed the door, my fingers scrambling for the lock button.

When he chased after me, I panicked and pressed a random button on the door's armrest, which rolled down one of the back seat windows.

Cursing under my breath, I pressed a second button. The car beeped right as Isaiah caught up to me.

"Hey." Isaiah yanked repeatedly at the locked door handle. "Don't do this."

I could tell by his tone that he meant those words not as a concerned warning, but as a threat.

*I'm sorry.* I clenched my teeth and jammed the key into the ignition. *But I have to.*

As the engine rumbled to life, I stared through the window, desperately searching for the brother I'd known so well. The brother who always compromised—who always put a limit on my trouble, but never stopped it completely. But that brother was no longer with me, and perhaps I didn't deserve him.

I backed out of the driveway, Isaiah stumbling away as the car slipped from beneath his fingertips. His chest rose and fell rapidly to accommodate for his heavy breaths as I set the gear shift into drive and creeped forward. I wanted to believe that he was giving up—that he was letting me get away with what I wanted to get away with tonight, but I wasn't so naive that I'd blindly believe whatever I wanted to believe.

As I reached a stop sign at the end of the road, I pulled out my phone and called Ari. She answered after only one ring.

"Jeremy?"

"Hey, Ari."

I held my phone against my ear, making a right turn with only one hand on the steering wheel. There was a bitterness to my greeting, not because I was still mad at Isaiah, but because I'd now directed my anger at myself. Not only had I done something so messed-up—so wrong—but I had also executed it so poorly that I'd been caught in the act. I had failed in more ways than one.

"Is everything okay?" Ari asked.

"Change of plans." I applied more pressure to the gas pedal, speeding down the empty road. "I know we said 3:00, but if we're doing this, we need to meet now."

"Now?"

"Now."

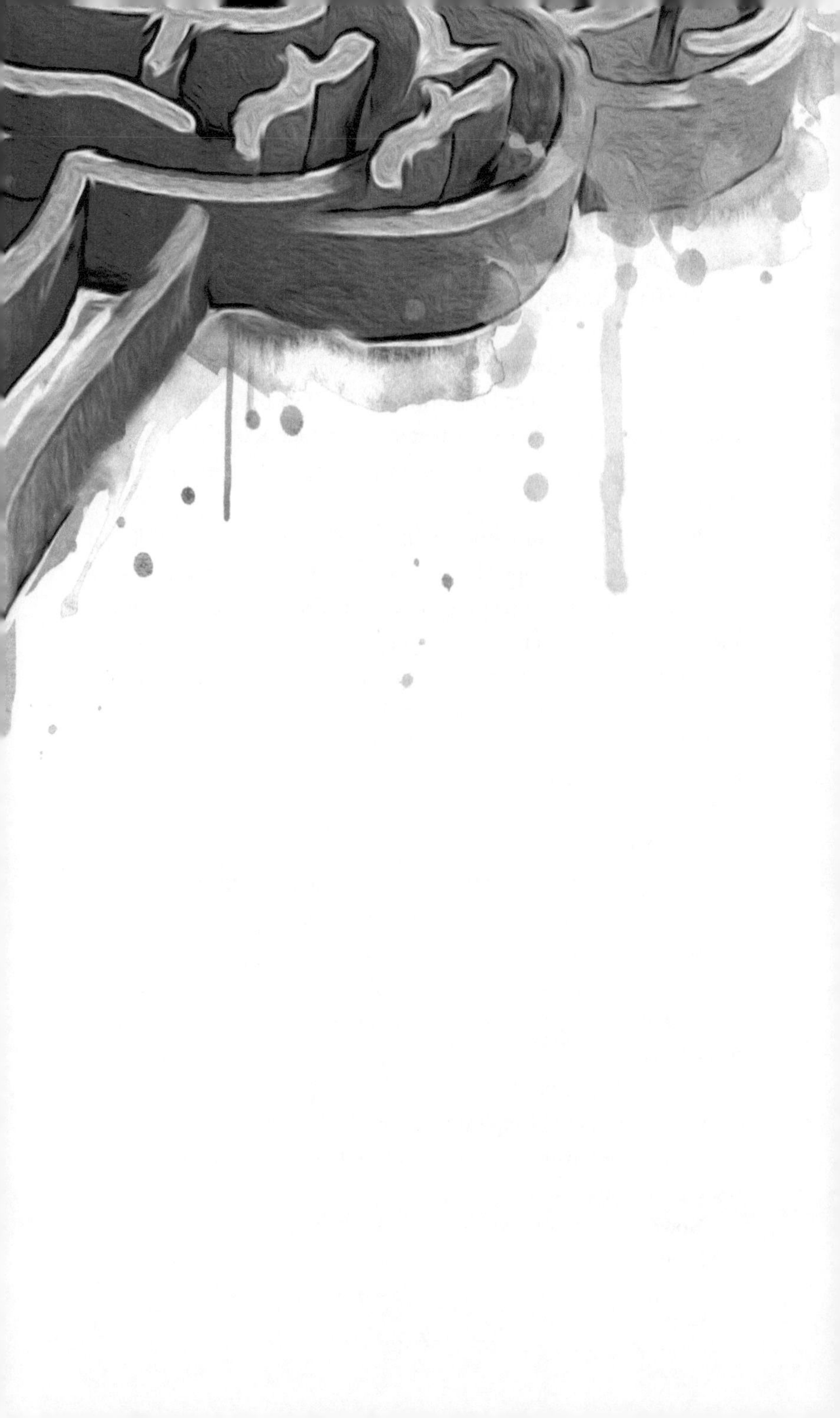

# ari

The streets were awfully eerie at night.

With my phone flashlight pointed ahead of me, I walked down the sidewalk by the Pentaware Art Museum. My eyes trailed back and forth over my field of vision in paranoia before I held my head low and made a right turn toward the front steps.

I was wearing a stupidly oversized magenta coat to conceal my identity in the security camera footage, and I'd even pulled my curly hair up into a bun and tucked it under a black beanie, just to be safe. Yet despite my heavy clothing, I shivered as a gust of cold wind struck my face, leaving my lips numb.

I dodged the front steps and made my way around the side of the building to the back, where Jeremy and I had agreed to meet. This end of the museum was far less impressive than the grand staircase at the front—nothing but a flat exterior wall and an empty staff parking lot.

I found Jeremy with his back leaned against the stone wall of the museum, eyes on his sneakers. He raised his head at the sound of my approaching footsteps.

"Could you have walked any faster?"

"It's your fault for changing our meeting time last-minute." I stopped in front of him and raised my chin to face twelve windows above his head —four rows of three. My eyes locked on the middle window of the bottom row—the window we'd chosen to smash for the grab. "Should I be concerned?"

"There's a convenience store across the street." Jeremy pointed toward the road next to the staff parking lot, and my gaze followed his finger to a dark building on the other side. "It opens at 4:00 in the morning. Figured meeting at 3:00 would be an unnecessary risk."

"Impressive." I reached into the right pocket of my jacket. "I've been taking some extra precautions too."

Jeremy broke into laughter as I handed him a pair of knitted gloves. "Don't you think this might be overkill?"

"Emphasis on *might*."

After sliding my hands into a pair of scratchy gloves, I reached into my left pocket for the two pairs of sunglasses I'd packed.

Jeremy shook his head, but he didn't question me before taking a pair for himself. It was likely that the outdated security cameras wouldn't get a clear image of our faces, but I wasn't willing to take any chances tonight, no matter how small.

"I've never felt like such a moron," Jeremy said, slipping the sunglasses on. "Congratulations."

I chuckled. "And how would you know that without your memories?"

Jeremy didn't give my joke even a pity grin. He flipped the hood of his black jacket over his head and squatted to grab the sharp rock we'd planted by our point of entry the day before.

"You ready?" he asked, and I could tell by his deepened voice that the mood had shifted.

Without waiting for my reply, Jeremy jumped from the asphalt and swung his hand against the window, the rock making contact with the glass. I slipped my own sunglasses on while the shards exploded from the wall.

He'd managed to knock out most of the window, nothing but a few remaining blades protruding from its sides. With a few more jumps, he struck at the surviving pieces, ensuring that the entire opening was blown out. And as those final shards fluttered toward the ground like shriveled leaves falling from a tree, my stomach twisted into a knot.

*Here we go.*

Jeremy dropped the rock onto the asphalt, and I tucked my phone into my jacket, preparing to climb.

*It's showtime.*

Although part of me felt like this was wrong—like we should turn back now and forget about this crazy plan—we'd come too far. After all, the glass had already been shattered.

*"Sometimes you have to push through the doubt,"* Jeremy had said the other day after I'd started to second-guess our plan. *"Just to see how it ends, you know?"*

He leaped toward the window, and I grabbed the bottom of his sneakers to help him up. After locking his elbows onto the tile windowsill, his shoes slipped from my grip as the rest of his body stumbled through the opening.

But even as Jeremy reached his arms back through the window, offering to pull me up into the building, I still couldn't fight my doubts away.

*Is getting my memories back really worth a crime like this?*

Tonight I'd finally remember my dream career, my favorite dish, and the reason why Stella had written for me to stop thanking her. I'd understand what my relationship had been like with Miles and why his existence had been kept a secret from me for so long. My parents would get their real daughter back, Stella would reconnect with the friend she'd lost during Remembrance Week, and everything would go back to how it should've been.

But regaining my memories also meant leaving the memory counseling group behind. It meant the end to planning schemes with Jeremy—perhaps the end to seeing him at all. Regaining my memories was the conclusion to everything that began the moment I'd woken up two weeks ago, and I wondered what I'd do next. Without a silly scheme like this to work on— without a mystery to solve and an old past to unwind—what would I do with my life then?

"Ari," Jeremy whispered. "We don't have time for this."

I shook my head to break the indecisiveness away and placed my gloved hands into his. After I kicked off the asphalt, he tightened his grip and pulled me toward the window.

*Now!*

As soon as I was high enough, I yanked my hands out of his and slammed my palms onto the windowsill. My arms ached as I used the last of my upper-body strength to press against the tile and propel myself into the building.

"Careful!" Jeremy shouted as I flew through the opening.

The sunglasses slipped down my nose as I clenched my eyes shut, anticipating my inevitable face-plant into the marble floor.

But my nose froze only a split second before impact.

I winced as my sunglasses crashed onto the floor in front of me.

"Thanks," I said in a breathless voice, realizing that Jeremy had grabbed my shoulders to prevent my fall. I set my hands and knees on the floor to support myself, and he released his grip with a sigh.

One of the lenses of my sunglasses had a crack running through it, but I slid the frames on anyway and jumped to my feet. My heart was pounding so loud I feared it might stop, but I couldn't pinpoint the source of my stress. Was it the fact that I'd almost crushed my face seconds ago, or was it because I was scared of bringing the old Ari back home?

*What if I don't like her?* I reached into the pocket of my jacket for my phone, which still had its flashlight on. *What if she's not the kind of person I want to be?*

As the flashlight illuminated the room in a dull glow, my worries vanished. Paintings with intricate golden frames covered all four walls, and handcrafted statues stood on wooden pedestals or inside elevated glass displays. Two arched passageways in the walls led to adjacent rooms with contents too far for my weak light to reach, but the pitch-black mystery only intensified my level of intrigue. Even with such poor visibility, the Pentaware Art Museum's interior was nothing short of magical.

*The first passageway leads to a room with an elevator.* My eyes flew from the first passageway to the second, which was located in the wall directly in front of us. *But the room through this one leads to the staircase.*

I'd learned how to navigate the building thanks to the floor plan Jeremy had drawn, but I couldn't shake a strange feeling of familiarity as I stepped toward the passageway ahead of us and into the adjacent room.

*Nostalgia.* I gripped my phone tighter as I ran toward the spiral staircase to our left, my eyes landing on a security camera in the corner of the ceiling. *Could that be it?*

Jeremy's footsteps followed close behind me as we raced up the steps to the second floor of the building. My feet moved with their own will as I followed the planned pathway I'd played out countless times in my head. I dodged glass displays and statues, stepping through various passageways until we finally arrived at our destination—the room where *Seahorse* was located.

I walked around the perimeter of the room, frantically waving my phone in the air in hope that the beam of light would eventually hit my target.

"It's over here!" Jeremy called.

I looked over my shoulder to see him standing in front of a painting near the only window in the room. There was just enough moonlight shining through the glass to make the piece visible without an artificial light source, and I instantly recognized the figure of a horse with a fishtail in place of its hind legs.

I joined Jeremy by his side only a few feet away from the wall and raised my arm to point my phone flashlight at the painting. The golden frame perfectly accented the blue swirls across the canvas, and a rectangular plaque hung next to the painting to confirm the artwork as *Seahorse by M.L.C.*

"Well?" Jeremy took my phone to free my hands. "What are you waiting for?"

I stepped toward the painting with a light grin. Although I didn't remember anything about Miles, I had a feeling that the old Ari had been proud to call herself his sister.

*It's smaller than I expected.* I held my arm against the bottom of the painting's frame, its width stretching from my fingertips to my elbow. *But it's just as wonderful.*

I reached for the left and right sides of the frame, but I couldn't bring myself to touch them. I was lucky to have an object from my past that was meaningful enough to bring my memories back, but what about the others? Why did I deserve this when Jeremy and Piper—along with everyone else who had fallen victim to Remembrance Week—likely needed this as much as I did?

"You've been working so hard," Jeremy said from behind me, sensing my hesitation. "You deserve this."

A sense of ease washed over me as my hands fell to my sides. Jeremy always knew exactly what to say to calm my nerves. Without him, I didn't know whether I'd have the guts to follow through with this plan in the first place. If anyone deserved their memories back the most, it was him, and I made a promise to myself in that moment that I'd do everything in my power to help him find his memories next.

"Thank you for doing this." I turned my back to the painting and wrapped my arms around Jeremy, my eyes falling shut at the sound of his heartbeat. "And if you ever need my help, I'm just a call away. I owe you one."

A moment passed before he hugged me back with stiff arms.

"Thanks," Jeremy said, his voice strained.

I stepped away from him, and he redirected my phone flashlight to the oil painting on the wall as I finally grabbed its frame.

With a light lift, *Seahorse* came loose from its mount, fully trapped by nothing but my delicate grip.

Jeremy offered me no time to process what I'd done. He rushed toward the nearest passageway, retracing our steps back to the room with the staircase. I chased after the stream of light that spouted from my phone in his hands, each step faster than the last.

By the time I finally arrived at the staircase, Jeremy was already halfway to the first floor.

*Slow down, will you?*

"Hurry up," Jeremy called, as though he'd read my mind.

I finally caught up to him by the broken window, where he'd been waiting with my phone held out in my direction.

"Let's swap," he said.

I studied his face, taking my phone from him as he took the painting from me. I'd always thought that I'd been the paranoid one, but he was acting as though the nonexistent alarms were blaring.

*This shouldn't be my concern right now.*

I climbed through the opening, lowering myself down the side of the building until I was dangling with my fingers clinging to the windowsill. With a tense jaw, I let my hands go limp and fell the short distance, my soles burning as my boots made impact with the asphalt of the parking lot.

Jeremy tucked my phone into the pocket of his jacket before holding *Seahorse* through the window and dropping it. I held my breath as the painting pummeled toward me.

*"Steal the painting during the next full moon,"* the anonymous letter had read, *"and your memories will return as soon as you leave the building."*

I caught *Seahorse* with a sigh of relief, and as I tightened my hold on the frame, my gaze drifted to the night sky.

*Any moment now.* I studied the full moon, waiting for my memories to strike as my mind drifted into a dream-like state, my thoughts vaporizing.

"Ari?"

I jumped, Jeremy's voice knocking me out of my trance. I'd been so lost in the stars that I hadn't noticed him land.

"What are you staring at?" He followed my line of sight to the moon as I searched my brain for the old Ari's memories.

But I couldn't find them.

*No, this doesn't make sense.* I raised the painting in front of me, soaking in every beautiful detail—every wisp of white and blue. *I followed the instructions perfectly. I stole my brother's painting and left the building, so why isn't the old Ari back?*

"What's wrong?" Jeremy asked, flinching as I thrust the painting into his grip. "You don't want it?"

*The letter was a lie.* A foreign rage coursed through me as I squinted at the shards of glass sprinkled across the asphalt. *And I believed it completely.*

I wrapped my gloved hand around the seahorse pendant at my chest, and for the first time, I hadn't done so out of habit or curiosity. I had grabbed that pendant with the hateful intent to wring out its every last breath.

*How could I have been so clueless?* With a firm yank, the golden chain snapped against the back of my neck, and I gritted my teeth as the broken pieces landed among the shards of glass. *How black does someone's heart have to be to write such a letter?*

And that's when it struck me.

*"Don't you think something's off about Jeremy?"* Piper's voice echoed through my head as I raised my chin to face the wide-eyed criminal in front of me. *"It's like he got his memories back."*

"You lied, didn't you?" I stepped toward Jeremy, my fingers rolling into fists by my sides.

He nearly dropped the painting as he took a wobbly step away from me, equalizing the distance between us. "Ari, what are you—"

"No! Don't say anything." My eyes burned, tears threatening to invade them as I stitched together the final pieces to the puzzle. "Not yet."

Over the past few days, I'd come to the conclusion that Jeremy and I were in this together—that we were a team. But the reality was that I'd been the lab rat in the maze alone, and he'd been the scientist. I'd simply been too blind to see it.

It was Jeremy who had planted the idea of stealing the painting into my mind. It was Jeremy who had written a letter to get my hopes up only to crush those hopes while standing right by my side.

"I get it now." My voice reduced itself to a mere whimper as I fought against what I knew was the only possible truth. "You never even lost your memories in the first place."

Jeremy shook his head. "You know I would never—"

"Did you really lie about your past and make up that stupid promise just to mess with me?"

"Promise?" His raspy voice smoothened, and he raised his brows. "Wait, what do you mean by that? What promise?"

The words in my throat vanished as I noticed the subtle reflection of red and blue in the whites of Jeremy's eyes.

We craned our heads toward the staff parking lot in unison as a police car pulled into it—lights lit, but sirens silent.

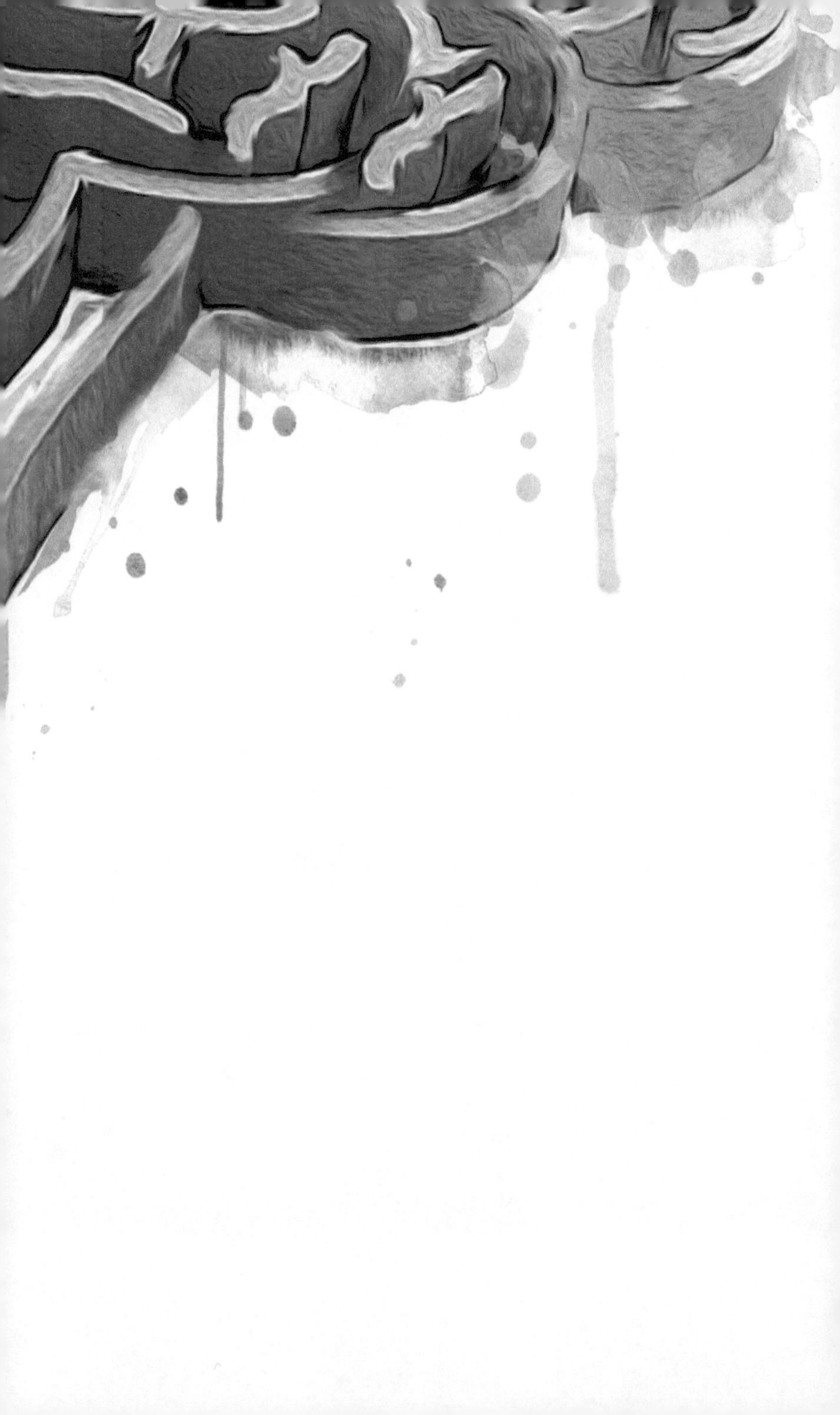

# jeremy

I sat in a dimly lit interrogation room at the Pentaware Police Station. It was the kind of room you'd see in a stereotypical movie scene, but the policeman in front of me wasn't bulky and intimidating in the least. He was blond with the face of a baby, and if he were to tell me that he was a new student at Damon Academy, I would've believed him.

"You're a lucky one." The policeman set his elbows on the wooden table between us, interlocking his fingers together. "No legal charges have been pressed against you, which may or may not be thanks to your family's hefty donation to the art museum tonight. However, I do have a few questions I'd like to ask before we let you go."

"What about Ari? Is she in any trouble for—"

"Because your friend is a victim of Remembrance Week, she's been given a *second* second chance."

*Second second chance?* I tilted my head as though that would somehow help me fit the pieces together, but I was at a loss. *What the hell is that supposed to mean?*

"Jeremy." The policeman raised his voice, drawing my hazel eyes to his teal ones. "Are you familiar with what Ari Cortez did three months ago?"

I blinked. His words had caught me off-guard once again.

"What did she do?" I asked, my voice frailer than I would have liked it to be.

"In August your friend broke into the Pentaware Art Museum to steal the exact same painting you tried to steal tonight." The policeman leaned forward, carefully articulating each and every syllable. "It was the work of her older brother Miles. The painting had been placed on display in the museum following his death."

"Her brother?"

*M.L.C.,* I recalled. *Miles L. Cortez.*

Although having her brother's art displayed in the museum sounded like a sweet way to honor him, I knew Ari had to have a reason for trying to stealing his painting twice.

"If you really didn't know about her past," the policeman said, "then why did you help her?"

Whatever lie I was about to tell this man I'd also have to tell my family to keep my stories consistent, so it had to be a smart one.

"Look." The policeman squinted, his icy blue pupils intensifying as he said, "We know."

"You—You know?" I could barely get the words out, my fingernails digging into my hand. "You know what?"

*Calm down,* I reminded myself. *It's panic that gets you caught.*

My eyes searched the room for something different to focus on, but when they landed on the policeman again, I froze, sensing that he was about to deliver the exact news I'd been dreading to hear the most.

"It was your brother who reported your plan tonight. He also told us about your memory loss fraud, which technically isn't a crime—but it is despicable. And for obvious reasons, you'll no longer be permitted to attend the teen memory loss counseling group here in Pentaware."

I stopped breathing, and in that moment, I didn't miss it one bit. I bet I looked like one of the creepy, life-sized statues in the museum, and the old Jeremy would've laughed to see me in such a panicked state.

"Why did you help her?" the policeman asked again.

The simple answer was that I'd offered to help Ari to distract myself. But the reason why I'd followed through even after my brother had caught me was much more complex. Maybe I'd started to view Ari as a friend, or perhaps my pride was too high to screw up two things in one night. But instead of choosing one of the many reasons circling through my mind, all I managed to choke out was one painful last lie.

"I don't know."

On our drive home from the station, the tension in the air was thick—too heavy to inhale with human lungs.

My father sat in the driver's seat with his brows furrowed, his lips pulled into a tight line. And his fingers—they turned white as he readjusted their tight hold on the steering wheel. The anger exuded from his face in a blazing steam, and I knew all it would take was one peep from my lips for him to explode and set the entire car aflame.

I clenched my jaw shut, staring at the passenger seat's backrest in front of me. Although I couldn't see my mother's face, simply gazing in her direction made me nauseous.

*I really messed up this time, haven't I?*

I wanted nothing more than to snap the car door open and fly out the back seat—to soar into the sky and escape from what I'd set off. But when the car came to a full halt at the stoplight—offering me an easy chance to run off if I pleased—a pinch of curiosity urged me to stay.

*Something's missing.*

I reached into the pocket of my jacket, pulling out the pieces of Ari's necklace that I'd gathered in a rush before heading to the station. The necklace was fixable—the chain broken but the seahorse pendant still intact.

*How could she possibly know that I lied about my memories? And why did she mention a promise?*

When my dad glanced over his shoulder, I folded my fingers around Ari's necklace and tucked my fist into the pocket of my jacket, hiding the jewelry from sight.

My parents hadn't uttered a word to me throughout the drive, and although I'd been dreading what they had to say, part of me was eager to get through what I knew was coming.

"You lied to us," my dad said, his voice so frail I hardly heard it. I avoided his eyes until the light turned green, sighing with relief as he reverted his gaze to the windshield. "Why?"

As the car picked up speed, I searched my brain for something redeeming I could say—an excuse that would leave my parents satisfied, or at least a bit less frustrated. I wanted them to know that I hadn't lost my sanity yet, but quite frankly, I wasn't sure whether or not that were true anymore.

"Apparently he doesn't know." My mom took a deep breath before raising her voice to a near-shout. "He doesn't know why he did any of this! How does that work?" She ended her burst of frustration with a sniffle, which confused me. I'd expected her feelings to match the anger her voice exuded, but what spread through the car was an emotion much more solemn.

"Your mom and I have been talking," my dad said, much bolder this time, "and we've decided it'd be best to transfer you to Deer Creek Academy next week."

"What?" My eyes widened at the realization that they were planning to send me away. Deer Creek Academy—a boarding school in Southern Washington known for improving the behavior of *troubled teens*. Rei and I had made jokes in the past about how we'd fit right in with the students there, but never in my life had I actually thought I'd be one someday. "You're kidding, right?"

"Oh, I'm kidding?" My father scoffed, and I caught sight of a slight grin on his face through the rear-view mirror. "You think that's all people do, don't you? They just lie and kid around?"

"You need this." My mother spoke softly now, but in a forced way, as though she were actively trying to water down my father's increasingly obvious agitation. "It'll be good for you."

"Because the tuition at Deer Creek costs more than Damon, right?" I nearly stood to my feet, but the seatbelt glued me down, trapping me in the reality of this new life I'd have to endure. "Because you think money can fix me?"

My dad's face turned red. "You know that has nothing to do with—"

"It has *everything* to do with the money!" I said. "It always has. You've never wanted to actually get involved with me and Isaiah."

"Then why is your brother normal, huh?" My mom was the one shouting this time. "Then why is Isaiah fine when you've caused us nothing but stress?"

*Then why is your brother normal?*

My mom's words had struck me like a dagger to the chest.

"Don't act like you're the victim here," my dad said before jamming his foot against the gas pedal.

My mom gasped as the car accelerated down the empty road. The red lights from the upcoming four-way intersection filled the night sky, seeping into our car and immersing us in a bloody bath.

For the first time in ages, my mind went completely silent, filled by nothing but the beat of my heart and the grumbling of the engine.

"Dad, it's red!" I yelled, finally able to part my shaky lips. "Stop!"

My eyes slammed shut as the car started to skid, throwing me forward. The tires squealed in pain against the asphalt, and the seatbelt dug into my waist to prevent me from slamming my head into the backrest of the passenger seat.

Everything went still.

I opened my eyes just in time to watch the air around me shift from a menacing red to a lime green.

My dad had struck the brakes too late, the car coming to a jagged stop in the middle of the desolate intersection. But even now, with the lights turned green, he no longer felt the need to race down the road. His hands fell from the steering wheel onto his lap as he leaned forward, his breaths heavy to suppress the rage that consumed his every muscle.

*This is all my fault.*

My eyes welled with tears as I yanked off the gloves Ari had lent me. I stared at my trembling hands, trying to will myself to stop shaking. This pressure had been here all along—always growing, always intensifying—

and I'd been dirt stupid for not realizing that my bubble would inevitably pop. That the rains would come pouring down and flood not only my own home, but the homes of everyone in the neighborhood.

A pair of words lingered on the tip of my tongue in the car that night. Two words I'd buried into the depths of my heart the day I'd pretended to lose my memories. Two words that could have saved me before all of this, had I woken up to reality sooner.

"I'm sorry," I said.

And I truly meant it. But I was too late.

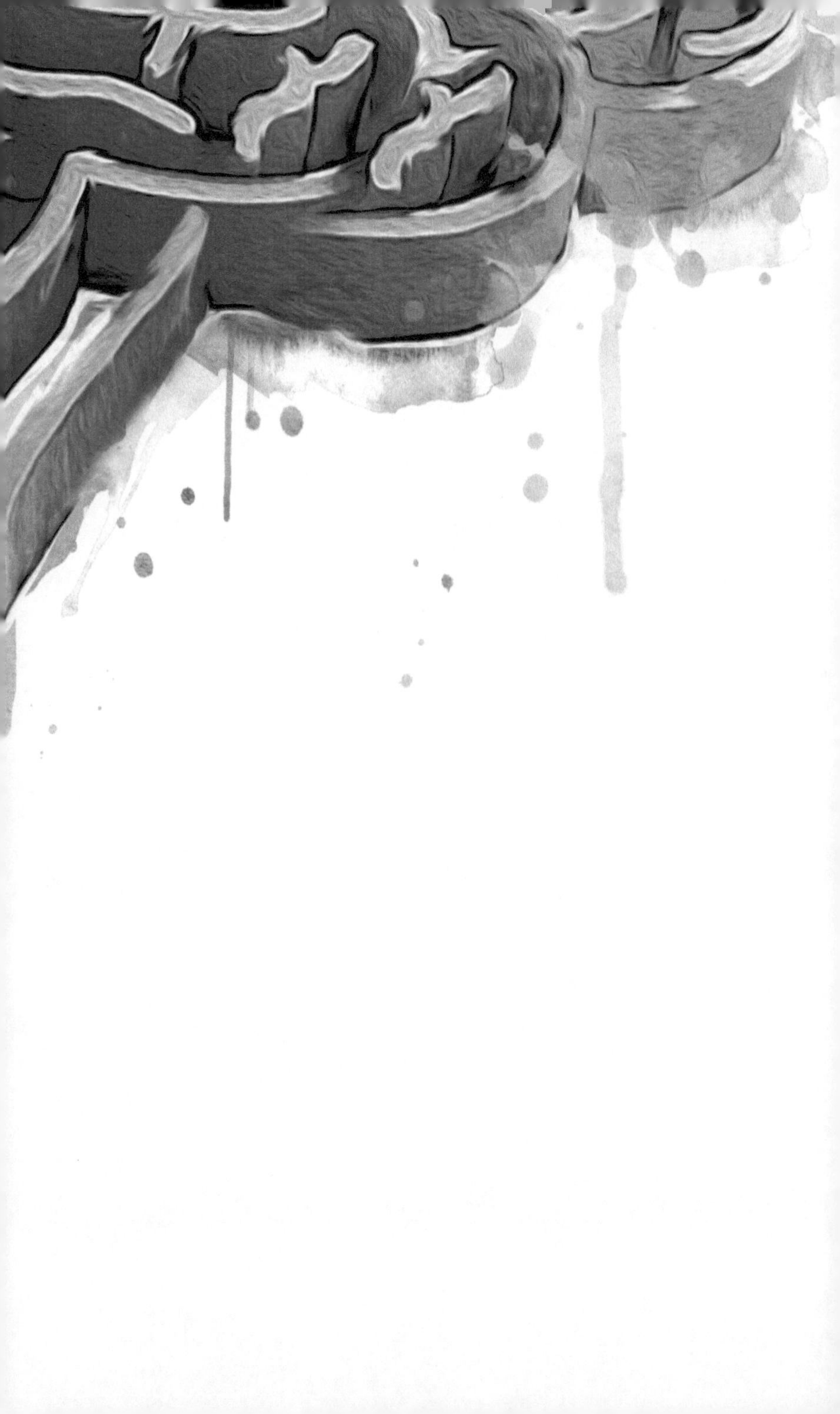

# ari

Our third memory counseling meeting took place on Saturday afternoon, the day following my failed heist. The ten chairs had been reduced to nine —eight memory loss victims, plus Emmett. Exactly as it should have been in the first place.

I sat in my downsized discussion group of now just Piper and me, fighting to hold my eyes open after a completely sleepless night. As I pinched my wrist to keep myself from dozing off, Piper shared her theories for Jeremy's sudden removal from our counseling meetings.

Nothing she said intrigued me because I already had the answer. Now that the police knew about Jeremy's memory loss fraud, there was no chance he'd be allowed to continue attending a government-funded program he didn't belong in.

*"For confidential reasons,"* Emmett had announced at the beginning of today's meeting, *"Jeremy Sargo will no longer be joining us."*

Piper paused to breathe, finally concluding her list of theories that I hadn't listened to.

"I don't know what happened, but it can't be good." Her dark eyes glittered even under the dull gymnasium lights. "I told you there was something fishy about that guy."

"True." I yawned. "You were right."

*And I was an idiot.*

I internally scolded myself for not listening to Piper when she'd warned me about Jeremy earlier this week. His change of behavior between the first and second meeting should have been a red flag, but the idea that his help could increase the chance of my plan's success had blinded me.

*I shouldn't have come today.* With a sigh, I leaned over and rubbed my forehead. *Now I feel even worse.*

This morning I'd insisted on attending the meeting, mostly because I thought it'd be nice to spend some time away from my parents. I wasn't openly angry at them, but it'd be a lie to say I didn't harbor any concealed resentment. They hadn't come clean about Miles until we'd arrived home from the police station, when I'd finally confronted them about his bedroom. Part of me wondered how long it would have taken for them to tell me the truth had I not pried for answers.

*It's fine,* I reminded myself. *At least you know the truth now. That's all that matters.*

According to my parents, Miles had been involved in a biking accident two years ago that resulted in partial memory loss. He'd never been the same after that, and he'd never been all that stable either. He would meet with a cognitive psychologist named Amara Singh twice a week.

*"According to Dr. Singh, art was the one passion that never left him,"* my mother had explained. *"Because Miles hadn't lost any muscle memory, he felt the most like himself while he was painting. Seahorse was all your brother worked on for months after the accident."*

I reached for my seahorse pendant, but my fingers met with nothing but the fabric of my beige t-shirt. I'd nearly forgotten how I'd ripped the chain from my neck in the staff parking lot of the museum.

*"You took it off today, didn't you?"* my father had asked during breakfast this morning with dark bags under his eyes. *"That necklace was a gift from Miles for your thirteenth birthday. His favorite sea creature—the seahorse."*

I was glad that my parents were finally opening up about the past, but their explanations had left out one crucial detail.

Any normal person would be pleased to see a loved one's painting on display, but this wasn't the first time I'd broken into the Pentaware Art Museum. Why had the old Ari attempted to steal *Seahorse* three months ago?

*"We don't really know why you did it,"* my mother had said in response to my questioning. *"But you likely thought it belonged at home with us."*

I found it a stretch to believe the old Ari was stupid enough to steal a painting with the plan to hang it at home consequence-free. Surely there had to be a stronger motive, and the fact that I couldn't figure it out left my blood boiling.

It was thanks to this anger that I jumped from my seat as soon as Emmett dismissed us from the meeting. I slammed the gymnasium door behind me on my way out, likely stunning everyone inside, but I didn't care.

My eyes stung as I rushed down the empty hallway of Pentaware High School. Last night was supposed to be the moment where everything would make sense, but now I felt more lost than ever.

I stepped through the front door of the building, and a chilly gust of wind blew by, rustling through my short curls. My lungs filled with the vague scent of caramel from a nearby cafe, but the pinch of sweetness in the air did nothing to lift my spirits as I ran down the front steps, eager to get home and sleep the next day or two away.

"Ari!"

A familiar voice froze me halfway down the steps, and I raised my chin to spot the plaid jacket I'd been avoiding for days.

Stella raised her palm in a shy wave, lips pursed.

*"On my wall I found a photo of the two of us. I'm pretty sure it was you who wrote it,"* I had mentioned to Stella only two days after I'd woken up. *"The note said to stop thanking you. Do you know what I was thanking you for?"*

I continued down the steps with my focus in Stella's general direction, but I avoided direct eye contact.

*"I helped you study for an algebra test once, so that might have been it,"* she'd said. *"You've always hated math. Not your best subject."*

With the light threat of rain misting against my cheeks, I acknowledged that I'd judged Stella too quickly. She'd withheld information from me, but I hadn't taken her own feelings into account. My parents had explained that it was Stella who'd helped me break free from the rut I'd hit following my failed heist three months ago. Surely that's what I'd been thanking her for.

And now that I knew the truth, I realized how unrealistic it was for me to expect a full explanation from Stella right on the spot. Both Stella as well as my parents wanted to break the past to me when they felt the timing was right. That's why Stella had lied, and it was for that same reason that two weeks ago, my mother had taken away the floor plans I'd drawn of the Pentaware Art Museum.

"Mrs. C told me what happened last night. You know, with that—that liar from Damon. I'm sure it's been a lot to take in." Stella stuffed her hands into her pockets as I walked down the remaining steps and joined her on the sidewalk. "Thought I'd walk you home."

I nodded, and despite my inner eagerness to tell her how sorry I was for cutting her off based on a small lie—for putting more trust in a stranger like Jeremy than a close friend like her—I couldn't bring myself to open my stiff jaw.

We pulled our hoods over our heads, the mist morphing into a drizzle. I could feel the tension in the air growing between us, and I knew the silence was my own fault, so after counting twenty of my steps, I opened my mouth to finally say it.

"I'm sorry."

But the words had come from Stella, not me.

"I should've told you about the painting as soon as I met you. About your brother. About all of it." Stella fidgeted with one of the buttons of her jacket, twisting it clockwise, then counterclockwise. I could tell by how loose the button hung from the fabric that it was a habit of hers, just as I'd often reach for the pendant at my chest. "Your parents told me that you weren't ready yet, and I couldn't disrespect their word like that."

"It's okay." I nodded, accepting that perhaps it really was okay. "You were doing what you thought was best for me."

I thought back on the letter Jeremy had left in the bush near my doorstep, and a pit of uncertainty struck me for the first time. If Stella had lied to me for a reason, surely Jeremy had too. As convenient as it was to call him crazy and leave it at that, it didn't make sense to assume that he'd set me up and faked his identity just for giggles. It couldn't be that simple. He had to have had a stronger motive, just as I knew the old Ari had a stronger motive for breaking into the Pentaware Art Museum than the simple intent to bring *Seahorse* back home.

"Did I really not know Jeremy before Remembrance Week?" I asked as we turned into our neighborhood. "Maybe the old Ari did something to him back then, and he wanted to get revenge?"

"As far as I know, you never talked to anyone from Damon."

"Hold on. I have a photo." I reached into the pocket of my jacket and pulled out my phone, swiping to find Jeremy's contact. Stella leaned over my shoulder, analyzing his disgusted face in the photo he'd taken of himself on Tuesday.

Her jaw dropped as she realized that his contact image resembled hers. "Is he—is he mocking my photo?"

I couldn't stop myself from grinning as I tucked my phone back into my pocket. It was nice to not be dead serious for a change, and I decided that for now, I was content with putting my Jeremy investigation on hold.

"I do have this other thing I can't seem to figure out," I said, my smile widening as I thought back on my first dinner with Stella the day after I'd woken up. "Do I actually like lemon chicken?"

It took Stella a moment to process my question before she burst into laughter—the hysterical kind that left her walking in zig-zags.

"No!" Stella shouted, her face turning bright red as she struggled to tame her humor. "No, you always hated it."

"Then why did my father—"

"You told him you liked it because it was *my* favorite. So whenever he'd make lemon chicken, you'd invite me over."

We stopped in front of my house, and I could tell by the spark in Stella's eyes that she truly cared about our friendship. For the past few weeks, she'd been making an effort to get closer to me again, but instead of appreciating said effort, I had pushed her away due to one silly lie of hers when I didn't understand the full picture.

"I'm so sorry for ignoring you," I said. "I never should've trusted Jeremy more than I trusted you."

*"Rule of thumb,"* Stella had warned me during our first walk around Pentaware together, *"never trust a guy from Damon."*

"Oh, stop. Don't you dare blame yourself for trusting him." Stella wrapped me into a suffocating hug for the first time in what felt like ages. "It was his fault for manipulating you with such a messed-up letter in the first place, you got that?"

I hugged her back even tighter, a wave of relief washing over me. I'd been so frustrated at myself for believing his lies when the frustration should have all been on him. Stella was right—Jeremy had taken advantage of my memory loss, using my longing for the old Ari to control me—and I had no reason to blame myself for his cruelty.

But just as I was finally starting to feel ready to move on—to finally put the past behind me and accept myself as the new Ari—a chill ran down my spine. My mind sifted through my memories of Stella from over the past two weeks, and I noticed that something was missing. The terror of what I'd discovered struck me with such a high magnitude that I could have easily convinced myself I was hugging the devil's reincarnate.

I pried Stella's arms off me and stumbled away from her. With every step she took in my direction, I took a step back, maintaining a solid distance between us.

"What's wrong?" Stella asked.

I shook my head, the rage terrorizing me in a way that felt all too familiar. It was the same rage that had struck me when I'd realized that stealing *Seahorse* would do nothing to bring the old Ari back—when I'd accused Jeremy of two unforgivable crimes when he had only committed one.

"Ari, are you—"

"I never told you about the letter."

"Mrs. C told me earlier."

I took an extra step away from her, my voice shaking. "I never told my mother either."

Stella stepped forward, closing the excess space between us.

"But I saw him do it." She raised her voice as though I'd correlate that with a rise in confidence—and therefore a rise in trust—which was not the case. "I saw him leave the letter by your house that morning."

*Wow.*

Stella was lying—and she was lying *desperately*. She knew it too, because her eyes dropped from mine to her muddied sneakers, admitting defeat.

I bit my lip, holding back my violent stream of questions. As curious and confused as I was, I couldn't take the lies anymore. The deceit. To know that there had been two traitors in my life left me helpless.

*If the best liars always have the most believable disguises, how can I trust anyone at all?*

I sprinted to the front door, ignoring the clamoring footsteps trailing behind me.

"Ari, wait!"

As soon as I entered the house, I slammed the door behind me and bolted the lock shut.

"Please." Stella pounded at the wood as I ran upstairs. "Let me explain!"

I barricaded myself inside my bedroom like a prisoner locking themself in their own cell.

With my back against the bedroom door, I scanned the wall above my desk. This collage was all the old Ari had left behind, but one of the most recurring faces in the film photos was a liar no better than Jeremy Sargo.

I had been acting with the belief that getting the old Ari's memories back would make everything right again, but maybe that was only a lie I wanted to believe.

Maybe the old Ari had been lost too.

I approached the wall, finally catching my breath as I reached for one of the many film photos. With a sharp exhale, I tore it from the wall and watched it flutter to the floor.

*Nothing makes sense.* I pulled down photo after photo, surrendering to the rage and allowing the uncertainty to fully consume me. *There has to be something I'm missing. There has to be something I'm doing wrong!*

I gripped an entire handful of film photos and quotes before ripping them from the wall in one explosive motion. They flew out in front of me, twirling through the air.

My violent fingers reached for another handful, settling as they pinched a single photo resting in a bald spot on the wall.

I didn't recognize the photo—and I recognized all of them—which meant it had likely been tucked behind a layer of other photos and quotes, hidden from sight.

My eyes widened as I plucked the stray photo from the wall. In it, my brother stood next to a woman who had her sleek black hair pulled into a tight bun.

I flipped the photo over to find a handwritten note on the back. The message had been addressed to Dr. Singh, whose name I recognized as the psychologist my parents had told me about—the one Miles would meet with twice a week.

"*Happy birthday, Dr. Singh,*" I read aloud. "*I hope you like the painting I made for you. In Greek it's called a hippocampus.*"

As I waited for my heart to stop racing, I wiped the warm tears from my cheek.

*I finally found you.*

In the mess of photos and quotes taped to my bedroom wall, I had uncovered a hidden truth—a secret the old Ari had left behind for me to find.

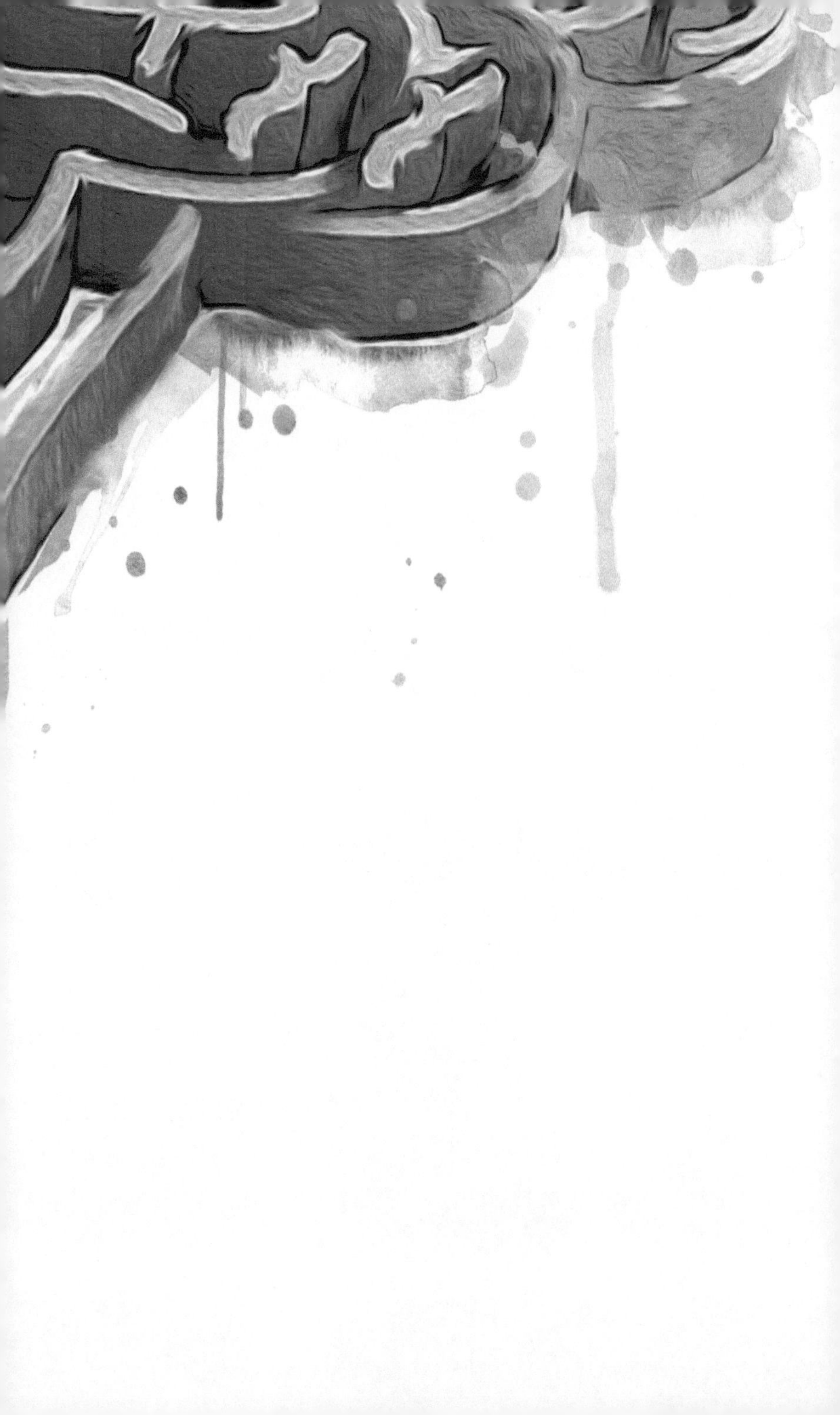

chapter 12

# jeremy

"Bad day?"

My mind was too muddled to make out what the waitress had asked me. I peeled my cheek from the sticky booth table and rubbed my sore eyes. "Just a coffee."

The waitress walked off for my drink order as my phone buzzed in the pocket of my Damon Academy blazer, which I'd thrown on over my black t-shirt on the way out of the house for the sake of nostalgia. I pulled out my phone, and a brief sigh of relief slipped through my lips at the sight of Isaiah's name on the screen.

*I'd be dead if Dad knew I left the house.*

Isaiah had likely noticed my empty bed by now, followed by our missing car in the driveway. Although my brother still didn't forgive me for running off from him the other night rather than taking his advice and coming clean, I got the impression that he did feel sorry for me. Yesterday he'd even brought food up to our room when I was too bitter to go downstairs. Even after all I'd done, I knew Isaiah was too kind to rat me out for spending time alone during my final night in Pentaware.

I declined the call and sent my brother a quick text instead.

*I'll be home soon.*

After hitting *send*, I tucked my phone into the pocket of my blazer and leaned over to rest my cheek on the table again. Memories from Damon Academy flooded my mind. It was at Damon that I'd met Rei for the first time, it was at Damon that I'd come up with the plan to scam Dr. Singh, and it was at Damon that I'd proposed to help Ari with her museum heist. Damon Academy had been home to everything, and it was a shame to leave it all behind.

I'd miss pulling harmless pranks on our secretary. I'd miss that horrible smell of artificial lavender in the library. I'd miss rolling my eyes at the boring conversations my brother had with his friends in the dining hall. I'd miss all of it.

*But maybe it's time to move on.*

It was currently past 11:00 on Sunday night, nearly two days after Ari and I had epically failed our heist. I'd been forced to pack my bags for Deer Creek Academy earlier today in preparation for tomorrow morning, when my dad would drive me to the nearest airport. My life here in Pentaware had completely shattered, and I knew there was nothing I could do to fix it. No matter how many times I'd apologize or how many excuses I'd make, nothing could retract from the impact of the lies I had told.

I'd impulsively snuck out of the house with the car keys to drive myself to Ruby's Diner. I'd been trapped indoors all weekend with a family that struggled to even look at me, and I'd never been so desperate for alone time before.

If the image of me sitting by myself in the only restaurant open twenty four hours a day in town isn't enough of a sign that I'd reached rock bottom, I don't know what else to tell you.

The waitress set a classic red Ruby's mug in front of my face. My stomach rumbled as I watched the steady stream of coffee spill from the pot, coming to a quick stop nearly at the brim.

As the waitress walked away once again, I raised my heavy head and straightened my spine, reaching for the stainless steel container of cream by the salt and pepper shakers that had likely been sitting there all day.

Rumor has it that Ruby's never throws out old cream, but at this point my life was so dull that I'd welcome even the worst of sicknesses.

When my eyes landed on a familiar face a few booths ahead of me, I nearly poured the cream right onto the table. I knew for certain that the blonde girl in the plaid jacket was none other than Stella Pierce.

I had seen her photo appear on Ari's phone after our second counseling meeting on Tuesday, and although Stella's hair had been short in the photo when she now had two long braids resting over her shoulders, I'd recognized her instantly.

Stella leaned over a milkshake in front of her, lazily sipping through the straw with her elbow on the table and her chin cradled in her palm.

I gulped and turned my eyes away.

*So that's Ari's best friend.*

As I grabbed a spoon and stirred my coffee, I lifted my chin ever so slightly to get another glance at her—just to make sure I wasn't imagining it.

*What the hell is she doing here so late?*

My stares earlier had likely activated Stella's paranoia, because when I looked at her again—my hand still subconsciously stirring the cream into my coffee—her chin shot up from her palm, and the straw dropped from her lips.

They say that time stops in moments like this, but honestly, I had never felt time rush by so quickly. I felt as though I had been staring at Stella for hours—as though a billion people had walked in and out of Ruby's, letting in a constant stream of cold autumn air. Stella and I sipped our drinks in silence, holding eye contact, but hesitating to break it with words, and after what felt like a lifetime, I was almost finished with my coffee, and she was almost finished with her milkshake.

"Something tells me you're not a memory loss victim." Her voice was louder than I'd expected it to be, purposefully amplified to ensure I could hear her over the two booths sitting between us.

"What gave it away?" I took another sip of my watery coffee, unsure of whether she'd intended for that statement to amuse me or not. "And how do you recognize me?"

A subtle grin crossed her lips as she left her booth and walked toward me, milkshake glass in hand.

"Ari showed me a photo of you on her phone"—she took a seat on the opposite side of my table—"which I found quite offensive, by the way."

I recalled how I'd typed my number into Ari's phone last week, copying Stella's disgusted expression for my contact photo. It'd been funny at the time, but my own humor didn't amuse me anymore.

"Are you going back to Damon tomorrow?" she asked.

I wasn't in the mood to answer that question, so I raised my mug to take another sip of coffee.

But I had none left.

"You know," I said, setting my empty mug down, "you're the last person I expected to see here."

"Yet somehow"—she set her elbow on the table—"I'm not surprised to see you."

The waitress briefly returned to refill my coffee as Stella took another sip of her chocolate milkshake. I reached for the cream container, my mug steaming again.

"What are you doing here, Stella?" I poured more cream into my mug with wide eyes, shocked by my own harsh tone. "Shouldn't you be cheering Ari up or something?"

She laughed, her head yanking away from the straw. The smile never faded from her face, even as she broke into a fit of coughs.

I frowned. "What?"

She grabbed a spoon resting on a napkin and twisted the handle between her thumb and forefinger. "It's just ironic, that's all."

"What's ironic?"

"That both of us screwed up in the worst possible way." Stella pushed her chocolate shake away from her with the tip of her spoon.

"I doubt that whatever you've done could possibly compare..."

I trailed off as she raised her brows, challenging me.

"Oh really?" I asked before setting my mug aside, losing interest in what minutes ago had been my only source of comfort. "Guess we both have our secrets. Do tell."

"I guess we do." She pointed her spoon at me. "You first."

"Alright." I hummed to myself, trying to pinpoint where to begin. "Well, my friend Rei lost his memories, and I went a little research crazy."

Sharing my side of the story made me sound even more stupid than I'd sounded in my head, but I must admit that it was nice to finally share my thoughts aloud. For the past few weeks, I hadn't even been honest with myself, so I sat at that Ruby's booth and poured my entire heart out that night. I didn't realize until a million words later that I was likely oversharing.

There was something effortless about talking to Stella. She acted as though she were constantly distracted, like she was listening just enough to hear what I was saying, but not enough to actually absorb it. She'd twist the loose buttons on her jacket or play with the utensils on the table, occasionally nodding along or making brief eye contact, but I could never tell if she was really listening or not. And perhaps that's what made it so easy. She acted as though talking to her were no big deal. Like everything I told her wouldn't be taken seriously.

When I finished explaining everything all the way to the end of the heist, she had emptied her glass of chocolate milkshake, just as I had emptied the stress that had been buried deep inside my head since the day Rei had moved away.

"Wow," Stella said. "That's pretty hard to beat, but I'll try my best."

I leaned against the backrest of the booth seat and nodded, clearly stating that I was ready to hear her side of the story.

She sighed dramatically. "Why do you think Ari tried to steal that painting?"

"Because it was her brother's," I said plainly, remembering what the policeman had told me. "Getting that painting back was important to the old Ari, so maybe she thought she could understand herself better by stealing *Seahorse* successfully this time."

"Actually, she didn't know any of that until after the two of you got caught."

"Then why did she break in?"

"Because I left her an anonymous letter with instructions on how to get her memories back."

I couldn't tell if I'd heard Stella correctly. "You *what*?"

"I told her that all she had to do was steal *Seahorse* on the next full moon."

"Why the hell would you—"

"Because Ari's always been a really secretive person, okay? She and I spent a lot of time together over the past few years, but we didn't actually become close until after her failed theft three months ago. That was the first time she'd ever opened up to me about something personal like that, and it brought us a lot closer together."

I ran my fingers through my hair, trying to massage my head into understanding where Stella was going with this. "So you—you thought you could get close to Ari again by replicating the same event?"

"Stupid, I know." She shrugged. "But in my defense, it almost worked."

I pressed my palms against the table, my cheeks burning. "So *that's* why she was so mad at me the other night. She thought I wrote that letter, didn't she?"

Stella nodded.

"Oh, you are just unforgivable."

"Ultra-unforgivable," she corrected. "Like, completely past the point of apologies. That level of unforgivable."

*Interesting.* My rage simmered down. *I guess we both know what that's like.*

All the hurt that I felt—all the guilt—it was inescapable, but there was comfort in knowing that I wasn't the only person who felt like this. That I wasn't the only person who had messed up in the worst possible way.

We had both wronged Ari. And although Stella and I hadn't known it before, our stories were connected. Perhaps they always had been—in some weird, abstract way. But I don't know. I've never been the philosophical type.

"So what now?" I said after a moment of silence. "Are you gonna try to make some new friends?"

"I don't think so." Stella placed the spoon she'd been fidgeting with on the table and crossed her arms. "Not until I know that I've tried my best to earn Ari's forgiveness. After I give her some space, of course."

There was something about Stella's eyes that I couldn't get off my mind. This strange glow—this motivation. She had lost Ari just as I had lost Rei, but instead of accepting defeat and telling lies to cope, she had done whatever she thought it'd take to rebuild their friendship—even if one of those strategies had been highly questionable.

And I realized that Sunday night—sitting in a near-empty Ruby's with the old Ari's best friend—that I had been living a life that wasn't mine, running from what I really needed to face all along.

Soon enough we had both paid for our cheap drinks and were eyeing the clock on the wall. The waitress kept looking over at our table—meaning she was either concerned about us or annoyed that we'd overstayed our welcome.

Stella and I shot a quick glance at each other, and we both knew it was time to go.

We stood in front of Ruby's Diner, about to head to our respective cars that sat on opposite ends of the parking lot. I felt a strange certainty that our paths had collided thanks to Ari, but only for a moment. We were simply two teens who had messed up at the same time and had found comfort in each other's mistakes, but now the light at our intersection had turned green again, and it was time to leave our accidents behind us.

Stella held out her hand. "It's been nice to meet you, Jeremy."

Without any hesitation, I placed my hand in hers and gave it a firm shake. "You too, Stella."

She leaned forward and lowered her voice. "Good luck out there."

Perhaps bad minds think alike just as much as great ones do, because she knew exactly what I was planning. I could see it in her eyes.

"Thanks." I smiled and released her hand. "Oh! I almost forgot. Can you give this to Ari for me?"

I reached into the left pocket of my blazer, pulling out Ari's broken necklace. As silly as it sounds, I hadn't been able to part with it for the past couple of days, but Ari deserved her necklace back, and what better person to give it to her than Stella?

She took the pieces from my palm and gave me a firm nod before turning around and walking away. I waited for her to look over her shoulder, but she never did.

The waxing gibbous moon guided me through the darkness as I drove mindlessly for what must have been hours. It wasn't until the sun started to rise when I figured I'd have to use actual directions to make it to Des Moines in a reasonable time frame.

*I promise to welcome Deer Creek with open arms.*

I smiled as I drove down a highway I'd never been on before, the horizon glowing with beautiful shades of pink and orange.

*But I have a quick detour to make first.*

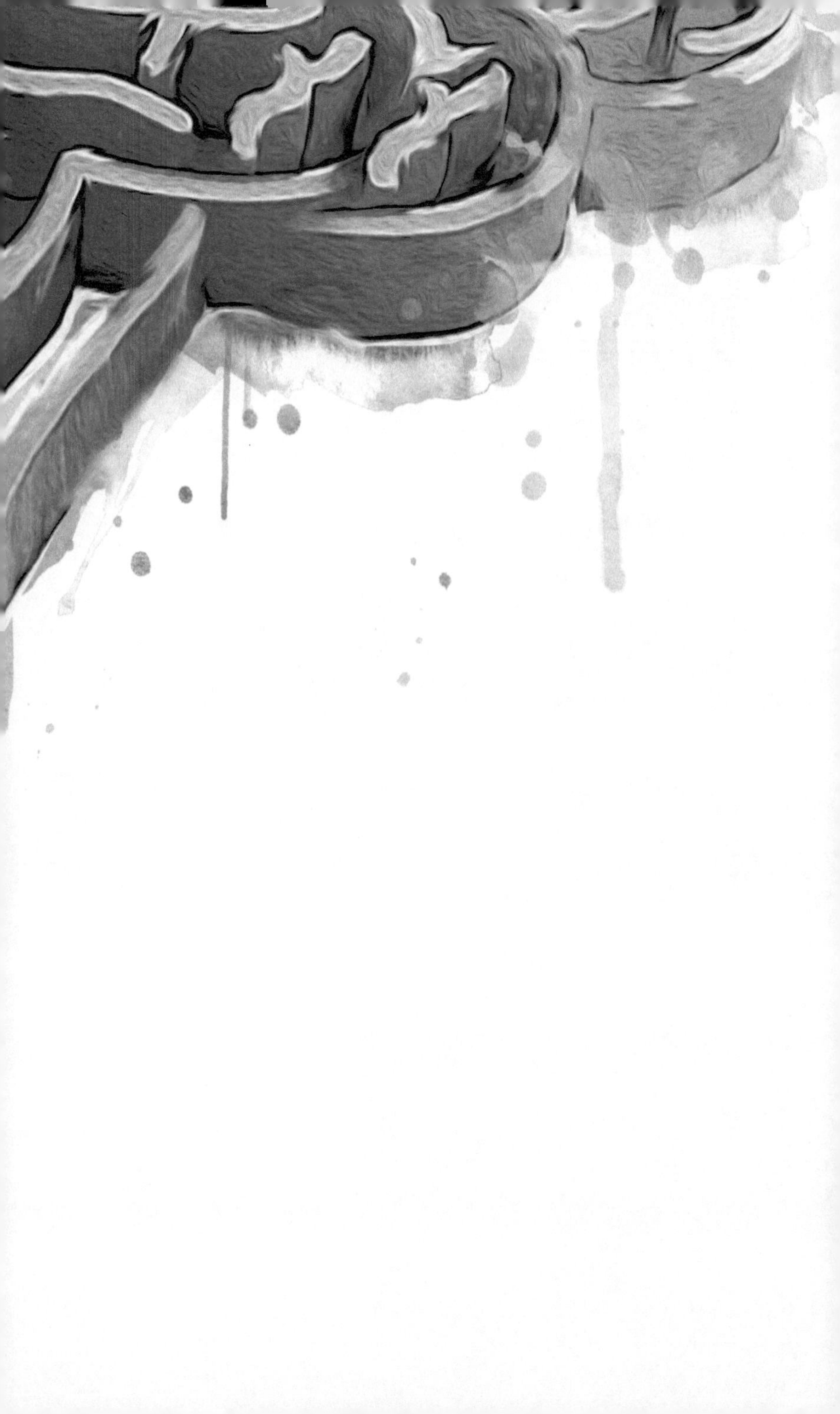

chapter 13
# ari

Two weeks after my failed heist, I sat on a bench in front of the duck pond at McCloud Park with the photo of Miles and Dr. Singh tucked into the pocket of my jacket. It was December 10th, not too far from winter, and the approaching shift in season was already starting to show. The colorful leaves that once filled every tree in Pentaware had now fallen completely, leaving behind nothing but wooden skeletons.

"Sorry I'm late."

I looked away from the swimming ducks to find Isaiah Sargo standing to my right. For a split moment, I thought he was Jeremy—which was neither a wish nor a nightmare.

Isaiah took a seat on the opposite end of my park bench, and I narrowed my eyes at the sight of a cream envelope in his hands.

"It's okay," I said. "Thanks for meeting me."

"Of course."

Yesterday I'd made a quick stop at Damon Academy during lunch break, playing the role of *Isaiah's cousin* so I could ask him to meet me at McCloud today. That must have been strange for him, considering how we hadn't spoken a word to each other since he'd denied me a ticket to the Pentaware Art Museum last month.

The longer we sat together in near-silence—only the quacking of ducks and the splashing of water filling the air—the stronger the tension between us grew. I knew it was technically my job to initiate the conversation, as I'd been the one to request that he meet me here in the first place, but I didn't know where to begin.

"I—uh—I'm sure you know that I was the one who called the police that night," Isaiah said, breaking the silence for me. "I'm sorry about that."

I could tell by the high-pitch tone of his voice that he was only half-confident in both of those statements.

"You did the right thing," I said. "But actually, I never knew you found out about our plan. I guess Jeremy wasn't as good of a liar as I thought he was."

"Yeah, I guess not." The bench creaked as Isaiah leaned against the backrest, finally loosening up.

"What happened to him anyway?"

I bit my lip, frustrated that I even cared enough to ask such a question. Although I'd discovered that Jeremy hadn't been the one to send me that letter, what he'd done was still horrible. Not only had he lied to me about his memory loss, but he'd lied to our counseling group as well as his own family and friends.

*"Thank you for doing this,"* I had said in the museum that night, my arms wrapped around him. *"And if you ever need my help, I'm just a call away. I owe you one."*

I scrunched my nose at my own words—equally frustrated by his lies as my own stupidity to believe them.

"My family sent him to a special boarding school in Washington. I think he's doing much better, actually." Isaiah fidgeted with his tie. "Believe it or not, he ran away a couple days after the heist."

My eyes widened. "Ran away?"

"He went to see Rei, one of our old friends from Damon who lost his memories last month. Rei's dad moved him to Iowa out of nowhere, and it all struck Jeremy pretty hard."

"I see." I dropped my eyes to my lap, and for some reason, I thought of Stella and how she'd written me such a horrible letter. Although I didn't understand her motive for doing so, I knew she cared about me. What if Jeremy was no different from her? What if losing his friend to Remembrance Week had somehow resulted in his twisted lie?

"So why'd you ask to meet me?" Isaiah seemed awfully eager to end the conversation about his brother, and I felt a bit guilty for prying in the first place.

"A few days ago, my mother told me it was thanks to a museum employee that *Seahorse* made it onto display," I said. "By any chance, do you know who that was?"

Isaiah flipped the envelope around in his hands around a few times, and although I caught sight of writing on the front, I couldn't make out any of the words.

"You may not believe this," he said, "but you and I met each other here at McCloud the day your brother passed away. It was a bit over a year ago, around the end of summer vacation, when everyone was gearing up for school. I was bored and decided to go on a walk just to get out of the house for a bit, and when I saw you here—you weren't having the best day, to put it lightly."

"So it was you?" I pretended to act intrigued, but I'd been expecting his answer. I'd realized recently that Isaiah had referred to me by name at the admissions booth.

*"Just stop, Ari,"* Isaiah had said after rejecting my purchase. *"I just—I can't deal with this again."*

At the time I hadn't thought much of it because I'd assumed that he was Jeremy—who knew my name from memory counseling—but I didn't remember introducing myself to Isaiah after waking up, which meant he likely knew the old Ari.

"Yeah, it was me." Isaiah nodded at my assumption. "Normally the museum buys art from these rich collectors, but I pitched the story behind Miles's work to the coordinators, and they were so emotionally moved they made an exception. They reached out to your family with the opportunity to feature *Seahorse* on the second floor. You were thrilled to see your brother's work on the wall."

"I was thrilled?"

"*Ecstatic*. We never talked much, but I'd see you at the museum at least once a week. You'd sit on the floor reading and listening to music in front of *Seahorse* for hours. It wasn't until three months ago when you came to the museum demanding we take the painting down. And when our manager explained that the art had been donated by the Cortez family—that there were now legal barriers that came with selling the piece back—you resorted to breaking in. And I never understood your sudden change of heart."

I reached into the pocket of my jacket, my fingers pinching the photo that had given me a look into the old Ari's ambition.

"Get ready for this." I glanced back and forth between Isaiah and my pocket, gesturing with my eyes. "It's a cool one."

Isaiah set the envelope next to him on the wooden bench as I pulled the photo out of my pocket. He took it from me to examine the faces closer.

"Turn it." I moved my pointer finger in a circular motion.

He flipped the photo around, revealing the message Miles had written. "Wait, are you saying that *Seahorse* was a birthday gift for Dr. Singh?"

I nodded.

He pointed at Dr. Singh's face in the photo. "Believe it or not, I happened to visit her office not too long ago, and she had a reproduction of *Seahorse* on her wall."

"A reproduction?" I didn't know anything about that kind of process. "How?"

"We have artists who come in all the time to paint reproductions. With more modern works like *Seahorse* they're technically not allowed to sell them for profit, because it'd be going against copyright, but I guess nothing would stop Dr. Singh from privately hiring someone to make a reproduction for her. I don't know. It's kind of murky water, but that's likely what happened."

"Well, I'm glad she at least has the reproduction." I met eyes with Isaiah, and he pursed his lips, a sign that he'd seen through my fake sincerity. "But the *original* belonged to Dr. Singh."

Thanks to this photo, I finally understood why the old Ari had broken into the Pentaware Art Museum. She'd likely discovered it somewhere among Miles's old things only to be horrified that the painting had ended up in the wrong place.

"I can't believe I'm saying this"—Isaiah studied the photo of Miles and Dr. Singh as though it were some kind of code he had to decipher—"but third time's a charm, right?"

He offered the photo back to me, and I took it with a tense hand, not sure where he was going with this.

"Look, I know Jeremy doesn't always make the best choices. He can be kinda—"

"Sloppy?" I asked.

"Yeah. Sloppy. If the two of you actually stole the painting without getting caught, you would've been the first suspect, considering your history with that painting in particular." Isaiah stared at the grass by his shoes. "But what if we... I don't know..."

I couldn't conceal my open-mouth grin, anticipating what Isaiah was about to say. "What if we *what?*"

He sighed into a smile, and his eyes met with mine again. "What if we swap them?"

I chuckled, shaking my head as I tucked the photo of Miles and Dr. Singh back into the pocket of my jacket. It was an unbelievably flawless plan. A golden opportunity to make things right.

"I doubt anyone in the museum would be able to tell the difference between the reproduction and the original," Isaiah continued in a tone that almost reminded me of Jeremey during our planning sessions. "I have a key to the security room, so I can get those cameras turned off. It shouldn't be too much of a challenge to take the reproduction from Dr. Singh's office either. I have a hunch that she's not always strict about following the law." He paused, his eyes searching my face for approval, which I thought would've been stupidly obvious to see. "So? What do you think?"

"What do I think?" My eyes widened, still in shock that Isaiah—the boy who had reported my last attempt to steal *Seahorse*—was now suggesting a more efficient plan to do so. "I think you're perfect, is what I think!"

Isaiah laughed as he grabbed the envelope by his side and passed it to me.

"This is for you, by the way."

I took the envelope with raised brows, suddenly curious again. I'd completely forgotten that he'd brought it with him in the first place.

Unlike the first mysterious envelope I'd received—the one that Stella had used to send me on a wild goose chase after memories I had now accepted were unrecoverable—this one had a return address in the upper left corner and a stamp in the upper right.

"It's from Jeremy," Isaiah added. "I found it in our mailbox yesterday. He doesn't have your address, so I think he wanted me to pass it on to you."

I set the envelope on my lap, not sure how I felt about receiving such a letter.

Isaiah must have sensed my discomfort, because he cleared his throat and hopped into another subject.

"You aren't wearing your necklace today," he said. "It was a gift from Miles, right?"

"I lost it." My free hand reached for the fabric of my shirt, right where the seahorse pendant would normally hang. I hadn't done that in days. "But yes, my brother gave it to me as a birthday present."

"I'm sorry."

"It's fine, really." I dropped my hand with a grin. "I'll never know my brother like the old Ari had, so I've decided to remember him in my own ways."

I sat at the only available table in Fire Roasters, a bustling coffee shop a few blocks away from McCloud Park. Isaiah and I had split ways, agreeing to discuss the details of our painting swap later. Honestly, I couldn't wait. Part of me missed the thrill that came with having a bizarre problem to fix.

I took a sip of my scorching-hot caramel latte, savoring the drink in sweet anticipation of opening the envelope Jeremy had mailed me, which still sat delicately in my hands, completely sealed. Or maybe I was taking small sips of my coffee in fear of what his message inside might say, just as I'd walked painfully slow on the way to Fire Roasters from McCloud. Anticipation, or procrastination? I wasn't sure.

I faced the brick fireplace to my right as the flames roared and crackled, urging me to rip the envelope open—to get it over with already.

So I did.

*Dear Ari Cortez,*

*You've been granted a second chance to get your memories back.*

*Just kidding. This one's from Jeremy, not Stella.*

*I know this doesn't justify what I've done, but I never lied to hurt anyone, especially you. I was trying to distract myself from losing a friend, but my lies formed a rabbit hole that only deepened every day.*

*Things were chaotic with my family for a bit, but I'm finally settling in at my new school in Washington. Deer Creek isn't quite as hellish as I though it'd be. I can definitely say that the students here are a million times more interesting than the guys at Damon.*

*I'm really sorry for what I did, but I'm not writing this to ask for your forgiveness. I know I don't deserve it. I'm writing this to thank you, because if it weren't for our silly plan to steal that horse-fish painting, I don't think I would've found the closure I needed. I hope you found what you've been searching for too.*

*Goodbye, Ari. And by the way, Stella has your necklace.*

I sat there rereading the letter over and over, the fire burning my right cheek. Jeremy hadn't run away because he wanted the easy way out, just like he always had, but because he wanted a resolution with his old friend Rei.

He'd left to reconnect, just like Stella had always tried to reconnect with me, and I'd be lying if I said that a part of me didn't respect that.

*Is this forgiveness?* My grip on his letter tightened. *No, not quite.*

The lies Jeremy had told everyone were unacceptable, but if there was one thing I'd learned from the chaos of November, it was that people always lie for a reason, and those reasons aren't always horrible. I didn't know if I could ever be friends with Jeremy after what he'd done, but as the fire started to literally roast my right cheek, I realized that I was ready to let go of my frustration.

Our paths had crossed for one week of November, and that was all there was to it. We were two teenagers stuck in the past—obsessed with it, unable to move on. But now I'd chosen to finish what the old had Ari started by swapping the *Seahorse* paintings—not because it's what *she* would do, but because it's what *I* wanted to do. I was done trying to become the old Ari, and from the letter Jeremy had sent me, it seemed like he was ready to move on from Remembrance Week too.

We were living our new lives now—lives that were no longer intertwined. In a year or two we might even see each other as strangers. We were the same as any other two people deciding which parts of the past to keep, and which parts to leave behind.

*Thank you.* I refolded the letter and stuffed it inside the envelope. *I have found what I've been searching for.*

Today had offered me a beautiful sense of closure, likely similar to the one I imagined Jeremy had felt when he'd reunited with Rei. I finally knew the ending to the story of my temporary partner in crime, and now I had no reason to care about his life anymore.

This feeling I had—it was easier than forgiveness, kinder than rage, and left me happier than I would have been had I chosen to pity him, or miss him, or wish that everything had worked out differently.

I tossed the envelope into the fireplace.

*Goodbye, Jeremy.*

As the flames devoured his letter, the heat against my right cheek grew unbearable, so I walked around the walnut table and sat on the opposite side. My lips curved into a smile as I reached for the phone in my pocket.

*Hey Stella*, I typed. *I want my necklace back.*
Which was a lie—but not the kind with bad intentions.

125

# Get $\mathfrak{L}$ost. in bonus content for
## *Memory Minefield*

Explore deleted scenes, author interviews, artwork, and more

L O S T I S L A N D P R E S S . C O M

# a c k n o w l e d g m e n t s

Sending gratitude to James Hensley, whom I've written this novella in memory of. His adoration for literature and his appreciation for my first two novels will forever motivate me to improve my craft.

Thank you to the other members of my family—especially Mom, Dad, and John—for supporting my passion for writing from a young age.

I would also like to thank my talented friends for their kind encouragement over the years—Joy Kabigting, Brandon Nguyen, Angie Eggers, Eliza Negrete, Sebastian Delgado, Abigail Ann, and Molly Jesus.

Shout out to the publishing team at Lost Island Press, including Katie Flanagan, Nora Sun, Sowon Kim, and Ratra Adya Airawan.

And last but definitely not least, thank you to my beta readers who read an early version of this novella and provided constructive criticism—Alexis Paucar, Germaine Han, Luis Rodrigues, Vanessa, Beka Lynne, Shelly Aarsen, Brian Goss, Paris Whitman, Nayra, Mirai Amor, Sydney Epstein, Pavani Gunnam, Kritisha, Nidhi Mathew, Anushka Jade, Chelsea-Rose, Christian de Souza Moreira, Ayesha Arya, Angeline Sieman, Jesmin Maria, Nicole Dust, Geoffrey Nadar, Halen Lock, Yo Deveras, 444, Raphaella Pasas, Lexie Johnson, Isaac Jaramillo, Blair Rossi, Saumya Babbar, and beta readers who chose to remain anonymous.

# also by mel torrefranca

## nightshade academy
### belladonna, book 1

Twenty teenagers are selected for an elite military boarding
school, but only five will emerge as guardians—destined for
a life of glamour and brutality.

## capsule

When a menacing app called Capsule auto-installs onto
Jackie's phone, she enters a game interlaced with reality
—a game threatening to kill.

## leaving wishville

Ten years after his father's disappearance, Benji plans to
escape from his self-isolated coastal town—but leaving
Wishville may cost him his life.

# about the author

mel torrefranca is a full-time author and founder of Lost Island Press. Her books feature morally gray characters, bold endings, and a pinch of awkward humor. Mel discovered her passion for writing at the age of seven and published her debut novel, *Leaving Wishville*, during high school. She also drinks way too many lattes.

meltorrefranca.com

# also from lost island

## my brother's spare
### shira behore

Valeria's secret investigation to find her mother's murderer
pulls her into an alliance with Alias Black, the most
infamous hitman in the kingdom.

## the memory jumper
### amanda michelle brown

Adelaide, an illegal Memory Jumper, lives in an
underground safe house with a narcissistic mother who
secretly exploits her mind-altering powers for money.

## lone player
### julia rosemary turk

To manage overpopulation, citizens are marked with
playing card tattoos—and an annual draw from a deck
determines who the Chaser Corps exterminates.

# about the publisher

lost island press publishes dystopian, sci-fi, and fantasy books. Unlike mainstream presses, we don't publish everything for everyone. We publish for *you*. Our catalog offers grounded, character-driven stories that linger long after the last page. The kind you get lost in, that keep you up at night. And because our books have the same vibe, if you enjoy one, you'll enjoy them all.

lostislandpress.com
join our newsletter for a free ebook

9 789898 501021 3